Simon Jacobs

PRAISE FOR *SIMON JACOBS*

'Beautifully written'
– Ronni Gurwicz

'An enlightening, devastating, but wholly uplifting read'
– Seb Jenkins, author of *Life After Death*

'The prose is simple, unshowy, yet still engaging. There's a directness to it that's refreshing'
– James Kinsley, author of *Greyskin*

'With rich character development and a keen eye for cultural detail, Joseph Estevez crafts a narrative that is both deeply personal and universally relatable. Simon's journey from isolation to self-discovery is beautifully rendered, and touches on themes of faith, social dynamics, and even the healing power of music'
– Joe Turner, author of *The Heart Collector* (*Alex Rainer* series)

'This book is an absolute gem. It's funny, exciting, and impossible to put down. From the very first page, I found myself swept into the world the author so skillfully portrays'
– Solomon Chambers

Also by the author

Poems
Poems, Book Two
Stories
The Calling
Isaac Abrams

Simon Jacobs

Joseph Estevez

First published in 2024 by Joseph Estevez

Copyright © Joseph Estevez 2024

All rights reserved. No part of this book may be reproduced or distributed in any form without prior written permission from the author, with the exception of non-commercial uses permitted by copyright law.

All characters in this publication are fictitious and any resemblance to real persons, living or dead, is purely coincidental.

ISBN 9798346618638

Edited by Tom Feltham

Author's portrait by Zion Yoni Levy

Blurb by Jake Waller

Cover illustration by Mark Swan

To Josh

Glossary of Jewish Terms

Ashkenazic: relating to Jews of central or eastern European descent.

Blech: a metallic covering over the stove burners to prevent cooking on Shabbat.

Chag: holiday.

Kiddush: the recitation of a blessing on Friday night during the Sabbath or on Saturday between the morning synagogue service and the meal. This can also refer to the light meal served at synagogue after the Sabbath morning service, before which kiddush is recited.

Gut Shabbos: a Yiddish greeting said during the Sabbath.

Gut Yom Tov: a Yiddish greeting said during festivals.

Havdallah: a religious ceremony that marks the end of the Sabbath.

Mezuzah: a piece of parchment with certain inscriptions that is meant to be affixed onto doorposts.

Motzei: used to denote the night after a specific date (e.g. Motzei Shabbat or Motzei Rosh Hashanah).

Parsha: weekly Torah portion read annually.

Parshat: see 'Parsha'

Shabbat: the Jewish Sabbath, starting from Friday at sunset to Saturday at nightfall.

Shabbos: see 'Shabbat'

Shul: Yiddish for synagogue.

Succah: a hut in which Jews dwell during the festival of Succot.

Zemirot: Jewish songs sung on Shabbat and festivals.

CHAPTER I

Simon Jacobs was celebrating at his house with friends and family. His friend from yeshiva in Israel, Chaim Spiegel, was there, as well as Rabbi Moshe Isaacs. He shared the house with Asher Wolfson and Naphtali Goldstein, who also attended the event. His twin brother and housemate, Reuben, was also there, as well as his parents, Mr Jacob Jacobs, and Mrs Miriam Jacobs, the latter of whom had brought homemade food. Reuben had also secretly attempted to bake a cake, the result of which had been a dish any cookery book in the world had yet to categorise. It had been quickly disposed of.

Had Mr Jacob Jacobs been given the chance to name himself, he wouldn't have opted for the alliteration. His father had begun a family tradition of naming firstborn sons that would be consistent with the lineage of the patriarchs. Thus, his grandfather had been named Abraham, his father Yitzchak, Hebrew for Isaac, and he found himself named Jacob. When his name was announced for rituals, he was indeed accordingly referred to as 'Jacob son of Isaac', a pleasure his father, 'Isaac son of Abraham', also enjoyed. Thus, Reuben, the older twin, had been rightly named Reuben, and Simon after Jacob the patriarch's second son. Reuben and Simon were not interested in keeping this family tradition, but for different reasons. Reuben intended to name his first son Abraham, after his great-grandfather, now deceased, in accordance with the Ashkenazic custom, as no one had been named after him and his grandfather Yitzchak was alive and well. Simon was uninterested in reviving the biblical naming in contemporary life. He couldn't recall the names of Simon of the Bible's sons, and he had already decided what his favourite names were, nor would he want to alienate his sons with uncommon names. He also secretly thought that his parents hadn't meant to keep the family tradition, but were simply lazy and unoriginal. Simon hadn't even been born in any of the weeks whose Torah portions concerned the life of his namesake; he'd been born in Parshat Yitro, which took up a section in the middle of the book of Exodus. Seeing that, after having Reuben and Simon, Mr and Mrs Jacobs had figured that that had been enough, and the childbearing and naming had ended with them.

Reuben and Simon were identical twins, so when Chaim, who wasn't so experienced in making the distinction, called up a surprised Reuben to speak, Reuben found himself improvising a discourse expressing how much he admired and appreciated his twin brother, which lasted for less than a minute. Embarrassed by his error, Chaim pretended he hadn't mistaken his study partner for someone else, then finally summoned Simon to speak, who spoke a little about the different concepts they had learnt.

They were celebrating a siyyum, the completion of a unit of Torah study. Simon and Chaim had completed the Gemara tractate of Chullin, which addressed Jewish dietary laws. They had spent the last fifteen months learning it, a feat that Simon found difficult to conceive. This had been one of the few things in which he had been consistent in his entire life. They had conducted their sessions over WhatsApp as Chaim lived in Israel. Because Israel was two hours ahead, Chaim would stay up late just to learn with Simon. They had decided to learn a Gemara tractate weeks after Simon had left yeshiva.

Simon was elated to see Chaim. He couldn't believe he was actually here in Golders Green. He had flown in Thursday night and stayed at his cousin's house, and they had been able to catch up in the days leading up to the siyyum.

As everyone conversed in the dining and living rooms, Rabbi Isaacs pulled Simon aside to have a word with him.

'Are you dating someone at the moment?' he asked Simon.

'No,' answered Simon.

'Are you interested in dating someone right now?'

'Yes,' said Simon, nodding.

'There's a lovely girl from Hendon, named Hannah. She's the daughter of one of my wife's friends. She's just arrived from seminary in Israel. She's twenty years old. How old are you, again?'

'Twenty-four.'

'Ah, so think about it. I don't know her so well myself, but I've only heard good things. Let me know if you're interested.'

'Yes, I am,' insisted Simon, nodding again.

Rabbi Isaacs, looking a bit shocked by his emphatic response, said, 'All right, then. I shall let my wife know.'

His wife? thought Simon, disappointed. This surely meant that Rebbetzin Isaacs would then tell the girl's mother before – and if she so decided – word would then reach Hannah. Why did it have to go through so many people? This would surely complicate things.

'Thank you,' said Simon, forcing a smile.

Rabbi Isaacs smiled back and nodded.

Simon was excited about the prospect of dating. He already held an office job at a local nursing home. He could work his way up to a more senior position before raising a family and living in his own flat or house with his future wife.

Asher approached with a glass of champagne in his hand. Naphtali followed soon afterwards.

'Mazal tov,' said Asher and Naphtali.

'Mazal tov, thank you,' replied Simon.

'I've always wondered how you are always so happy,' remarked Asher, reflecting the smile Simon had on his face.

'Look at that smile,' observed Naphtali, grinning too. He was much taller than Simon and Asher, and slender, with short, dark hair.

'I've got a lot to be grateful for,' said Simon. 'I've got my friends, family, Chaim, my home, my job, good health. It's in *Pirkei Avot*, that one who is happy with what he has is considered rich.'

Naphtali nodded, looking impressed.

'Well said,' said Asher.

The food had been served on the dining table in the dining room, though Simon's parents and rabbi were conversing in the living room.

Simon, Asher, and Naphtali were conversing in the corridor with glasses of champagne in their hands.

'How's the job going?' asked Asher.

'Well, I've still got it,' replied Simon, 'haven't got fired yet.'

Asher and Naphtali laughed.

'Thank God,' said Naphtali.

Simon was rather curious about this girl named Hannah. He spotted Reuben standing in the living room by Rabbi Isaacs. He went up to him, tapped him on the shoulder, and jerked his head towards the corridor, where they passed through, and they stood by the back door that gave view to the garden, speaking privately.

'Have you by any chance heard of a girl named Hannah from Hendon?'

'I'm afraid not,' replied Reuben. 'Why?'

'I may start dating her,' said Simon, finding it hard to believe that these words were now coming out of his mouth.

'Oh, well, I haven't. Sorry,' said Reuben. 'I actually might be dating a girl myself. She's in seminary now.'

'Oh, lovely,' said Simon.

'Yeah. I might get set up with her. She'll be arriving in a few months. It's still not official, though.'

The two of them returned to Asher and Naphtali, who were still standing in the corridor. The vibrant sounds of several conversations filled the house.

'Wow, so much musical talent here,' remarked Reuben upon seeing Simon, Asher, and Naphtali standing next to each other. 'How's the band?'

Simon thought it was a funny way to refer to them as a group.

'Good,' said Naphtali, nodding.

Reuben then left the group.

'Well, I guess we are a band,' joked Asher.

As Reuben passed through the living room and into the dining room, Simon noticed his used napkin sway as it fell from his emptied plate and onto the floor. He checked to see if he would pick it up. Seeing that he didn't, he fought the urge to do so to keep the floor clean, but he remained where he was to keep conversing with his housemates. However, they both walked over to the living room.

Simon then looked around for Chaim. It was then that he noticed that he had disappeared. He wondered where he had gone. He then picked up Reuben's napkin and threw it out into the bin in the kitchen.

He returned to the living room, which was when he felt like bringing out his acoustic guitar to play some music and entertain the guests, but it was then that Naphtali appeared with his acoustic guitar, and he started playing it while sitting on the sofa. Mr and Mrs Jacobs and Rabbi Isaacs paused briefly from their conversation to watch him play before continuing to chat. Asher and Reuben stood around in the living room, admiring him as he played.

Simon floated around the living room as Naphtali's music filled the atmosphere. He gazed out of the living room window and caught sight of his friend Dan walking down the street with a tall, slender young man looking to be around their age whom Simon had never met before. He expected them to enter the house, even though he hadn't invited the stranger, and Dan had said that he couldn't make it, and they ended up passing his house. He assumed he couldn't have made it because he had made plans with this other person. His other friend Yehuda had said that he couldn't make it either. He wondered why. He, Reuben, Asher, Naphtali, Dan, and Yehuda had all gone to the same Jewish secondary school here in London. They had remained friends ever since.

Mr and Mrs Jacobs came over and embraced him.

'Mazal tov,' said Mrs Jacobs, before Mr Jacobs said the same.

'Thank you,' said Simon. 'How's everyone doing?' Simon wondered why his grandparents couldn't have made it.

'My mother isn't feeling so well,' said Mrs Jacobs. 'But it's not so serious, only a cold.'

They and Rabbi Isaacs left shortly afterwards.

Asher approached Simon and asked him, 'Have you ever been to America?'

'No,' said Simon.

'Would you ever go? I've got a cousin who lives there in New York City. I'm thinking about visiting him sometime.'

'I don't know. There's quite a bit of gun violence there,' said Simon, 'and either way, I haven't got the money to go on holiday there any time soon.'

Reuben came over and confessed, 'Thank God. It was feeling a bit crowded.'

Chaim then reappeared, passing through the corridor.

'Ah, there you are,' said Simon. 'I was wondering where you were.'

'Sorry, I just had to leave for a minute,' said Chaim.

Naphtali stopped playing music. He and Asher then exited the house.

'Mazal tov,' said Chaim.

'Thanks,' said Simon. 'Mazal tov to you as well.'

They saw that the house had become quiet. Only the two of them and Reuben were there. The siyyum had apparently come to an end.

'Shall we go for a walk?' suggested Chaim.

'Certainly,' said Simon, wanting to finally catch up with him.

CHAPTER II

Simon didn't know when the next time he would see his friend again would be. After the walk, he returned home and found Asher and Naphtali jamming in the living room, Naphtali singing while Asher played the electric guitar. He couldn't tell whether they were playing some rock song he'd never heard of or improvising, but he enjoyed it. He listened to them for a bit before heading upstairs to his bedroom.

Chaim would leave the next morning. Simon felt the loss as he walked to work. He felt the whole country was losing amidst his departure, and he was willing to bear the loss of all sixty-seven million inhabitants of the United Kingdom, seeing that the vast majority of them couldn't have appreciated him for who he was as they had never met him.

He arrived at the office, and within two hours of working, he was summoned to his boss's office. He wondered whether he was going to get fired or get a promotion. He analysed his work productivity over the last several weeks as Mr Williams invited him to have a seat and close the door.

'I'm very sorry to tell you this, Simon,' said Mr Williams, 'but we're downsizing due to the state of the economy, and we're letting a lot of the office staff go. I'm afraid we're going to have to let you go. I am very sorry. You may stay until Friday, by which point I'm afraid you'll have to leave.'

Simon couldn't even think about the future, mostly because he no longer knew what it held.

'I understand, thank you,' said Simon. 'Thank you for allowing me to work here.'

'You are much appreciated,' said Mr Williams, looking regretful as he bit his lip. 'This was not an easy decision to make.'

Mr Williams nodded and looked down. Simon nodded as well. He got up and left the office, returning to his desk. He could barely focus. He would work until Friday; he needed the money.

Rumours circulated around the office about who had been and who would be fired. Simon confirmed thrice that he had been one of the lucky ones, to add insult to injury. By early afternoon, several of the chosen had agreed to help each other find employment elsewhere, but Simon remained silent; he'd never had a close relationship with any of his colleagues, most of whom were much older, and with different lifestyles, and he didn't know where he'd want to work; he couldn't imagine working anywhere else yet.

He was able to get some of his tasks done by the end of his shift. He had a headache as he walked home. He couldn't believe it. He was walking the five-day death sentence of his job. He wouldn't tell his parents; they were anxious enough already, and this would give them a panic attack every day until he was employed again. He'd wait until he'd find his next job, or at least when he was close to obtaining one. He wouldn't tell Reuben, either, lest he worry him as well, especially since he'd have to contribute to the rent, and the lease was under Reuben's name. At least, he had enough savings to pay for the rest of the lease, which would end on the 31st of December, and it was now the 21st of August.

He went for a walk around the neighbourhood, enjoying the warm, sunny weather. He thought about Chaim and the walk they had taken the previous day and missed him. He arrived home to find Reuben already having his supper, and he decided to make himself a salad and prepare pasta.

Reuben had moved into the house on the 1st of January 2022 when he had heard of the availability of one of the rooms. His three other housemates had been strangers to him at the time, other guys also in their twenties. At the start of 2023, they had moved out and the lease had been under his name. Simon had decided to move in. It had been a few months after he had arrived from Israel where he had studied at yeshiva and after obtaining his current job. As the other rooms had also been available, he had brought his friends Naphtali and Asher with him. So in a way, he felt particularly responsible for seeing that the rent was paid. It was hard to refrain from telling Reuben about his redundancy as he was cutting vegetables for the salad. He was not accustomed to keeping secrets from his brother.

That night, after the evening service at his synagogue, Simon noticed a new face amongst the congregants. He was a rather tall, slender man with curly brown hair and large glasses. He was standing still, gazing around, admiring the interior of the synagogue.

Simon thought it would be nice to welcome him, so, he approached him.

'Hi, what's your name?'

The man turned and shook Simon's hand.

'Hi! I'm Aaron Perlman. I'm guessing you're from around here, based on your accent?'

'Yes,' said Simon.

Aaron had a wide, friendly grin. His accent suggested to Simon that he was American. He seemed full of energy, seemingly excited to be talking to Simon, which he appreciated, though it did make him feel a bit timid.

'Where are you from?' asked Simon.

'I'm from Chicago. I came here not too long ago for school. I'm twenty-one. I'm just looking for an apartment.'

Simon nodded, his mouth open as he answered his question along with four or five others he had never asked.

'Are you liking it here so far?' asked Simon.

'Yeah, it's great! I just arrived yesterday, and I'm a bit jet-lagged, but so far so good.'

'Ah, lovely. Well, welcome. I hope you enjoy your stay.'

'Thank you, I guess I'll see you around, maybe on Shabbos or something.'

'Right,' said Simon, forcing a smile back to reflect his.

Aaron left, and Rabbi Isaacs approached.

'Simon, I've received word regarding Hannah.'

'Oh, great,' responded Simon, impressed by the rabbi's speed.

'She said she should be ready to start planning for the first meeting soon.'

'Oh, wonderful,' said Simon, becoming excited by the prospect, but still wondering how soon 'soon' would be. 'So, did she say when?'

'Not quite.'

'OK,' he said confusedly.

With every day that passed, the termination of Simon's job approached. He felt like he was being slowly suffocated. Then Friday finally came, along with it the last time he would leave work and embark on a road of uncertainty. Thus, upon entering Shabbat, he was jobless and worried about his financial situation, which made being joyous a lot easier.

CHAPTER III

After the Shabbat morning service at the synagogue, Simon noticed Aaron at kiddush, where the congregants stood conversing in small groups as they enjoyed snacks and drinks. 'Hi, Aaron, how are you?' he said, going over.

Aaron nodded, his facial expression neutral as he barely turned to face him, his hands in his pockets as he stood in the centre of the dining hall. 'Good, you?'

'I'm great,' replied Simon, wondering whether he was upset. 'Are you all right?'

'Yeah, I'm great,' he said confusedly, as if it wasn't necessary to ask.

'Oh, all right,' said Simon, a bit taken aback. Seeing that Aaron was avoiding eye contact, Simon assumed he wasn't interested in conversing.

Simon was a bit confused. Aaron had seemed so full of life and excited to meet him earlier that week. He had been hoping to get to know this newcomer better as he seemed interesting. Maybe the jet lag had caused him to be more animated and excitable, rather than fatigued and grumpy, and now that he was in his normal state, he didn't want to talk to him, an inhabitant of the country he was apparently trying to live in.

So, he accepted this. He saw Rabbi Isaacs standing in the corner with his wife. They were chatting with two women. He wondered whether now was the right time to ask if there was an update on Hannah. He wondered whether he'd come across as annoying or desperate, but finally decided he should risk asking. The worst that could happen was that he wouldn't have an update. It had been several days since they had last spoken about her. So when the two ladies had finally departed, he approached the rabbi.

Rabbi Isaacs appeared tense when he recognised Simon, and Simon assumed he had no good news to share.

'Simon, Shabbat Shalom,' said Rabbi Isaacs, reaching out his hand.

'Shabbat Shalom, rabbi,' responded Simon, shaking it. 'I was wondering whether there was an update regarding Hannah.'

Rabbi Isaacs bit his lip, nodding slowly.

'There is. I'm afraid she's not going to go through with this. She's decided she would like to go back to Israel to study at seminary for another year.'

Now she'd decided she wanted to study for another year? thought Simon. He wondered whether he'd had anything to do with it. Should he continue to accept recommendations before chasing every other single Jewish girl out of the country?

'I understand, thank you,' he said, forcing a smile.

'I'm sorry,' said Rabbi Isaacs.

Thus ended his hopes of ever being with Hannah of Hendon.

Simon left shortly afterwards. He and Reuben had a quiet Shabbat meal at home, where they had prepared various dishes for lunch. Asher and Naphtali were having lunch at their parents' homes. Simon and Reuben would often go to their parents' house for the Shabbat meals also. Throughout the meal, Simon brooded over his disappointment at Aaron's coldness and not being able to plan a first date with Hannah. He'd been looking forward to talking to Aaron and Hannah this whole week, but his expectations had been shattered – all within the same week of losing his job, which he had yet to tell anyone about. It was like the whole world was playing tricks on him.

But he remained optimistic. There was nothing he could do about Aaron or Hannah. The following week, he would search for jobs. He would have plenty of time to do so, and he was sure he would find a job soon. And there was something else he had to look forward to: seeing his friends tonight.

After Shabbat ended, Simon and Reuben headed to their friend Yehuda Levy's house, where they would have Melaveh Malkah.

'It's so hot,' complained Reuben.

'I'm so excited,' said Simon. 'We haven't been at Yehuda's house for a while.'

'You know the only reason why Dan asked to hang out there tonight is because he likes his sister, Rachel –'

'Sh. Let's not speak lashon hara,' said Simon, which meant 'evil tongue', or when one bad-mouths someone else. 'We'll have a good time and that's all that matters.'

'Just so Dan can finally get the chance to talk to Rachel? It's odd for me to watch.'

'So, don't watch, then. Have a piece of fruit, or start your own conversation with someone else.'

'I don't like being there,' admitted Reuben. 'I get a weird feeling from his parents, and I never know what to do in their house.'

'Talk to me if you don't know what to do,' Simon assured him.

'I hope we're not late.'

Simon checked his watch.

'Not to worry; we're five minutes early,' he said as they made a left and the house came into view.

'No, we mustn't arrive so early,' insisted Reuben. 'We'll be the only guests there! Let's come back later.'

Reuben stopped, and Simon did the same about a metre ahead. He turned around and said, 'What's the big deal?'

'It's just awkward,' said Reuben.

'No, it's not. Look, there's Asher and Naphtali coming up ahead.'

Simon raised his chin towards Asher and Naphtali, who were approaching from the other side of the street.

Reuben followed Simon and the others without another word towards the Levy house.

Simon knocked, and Mrs Levy welcomed them in with a grin.

They celebrated with food and music. Asher had brought his electric guitar, and Matthew Collins, a friend of Asher's who joined in their activities from time to time, was also there with his bass guitar. Simon would've brought his acoustic guitar had he anticipated the music, but Naphtali had brought his own, so at least it wasn't lacking. Dan Shapiro eventually arrived too.

They all partook of bread and refreshments in the dining room, where they mostly stood around chatting as Asher and Naphtali played their guitars.

Simon noticed that Rachel was chatting with some girl he had never seen before. He spoke with Matthew and Yehuda. Reuben stood quietly by the corner, a glass of white wine in his hand. Dan then joined their conversation.

'Who's that?' asked Dan, eyeing Rachel's friend.

'That's Hannah, my sister's friend,' replied Yehuda.

Simon froze.

'Where is she from?' asked Dan.

'Hendon.'

Simon felt a pressure expanding in his chest.

'Is her mum friends with Rabbi Isaacs' wife?' asked Simon. He knew it wasn't likely Yehuda would know, and it was an odd question to ask, but it was one of the few facts he knew about the Hannah Rabbi Isaacs had spoken about, and he was curious to know whether this was really her.

'Yes,' replied Yehuda, looking a bit confused. 'How do you know?'

'Oh, I may have heard of her,' said Simon, shrugging. 'Rabbi Isaacs may have mentioned something about her once – because he cares about the Jewish people.'

The suspicious looks on their faces thankfully dissipated, and Yehuda continued, 'She'll be going to seminary soon.'

'Ah,' uttered Dan, looking down in disappointment.

Simon had goosebumps. He couldn't believe it; the girl that Rabbi Isaacs had been talking about was standing just across the room from him. He knew it was her, but she couldn't tell it was him. He avoided eye contact at all costs. It was a lost cause; she was going to seminary – unless she had made up an excuse not to date him, for whatever reason.

Yehuda went to chat with Naphtali.

'I've noticed you guys say a blessing before partaking of food or drink,' said Matthew, who wasn't Jewish. 'Do you say the same one for every food and drink?'

'No, we say a different one depending on the food,' said Dan.

'Or drink,' added Simon.

'Ah, fascinating,' remarked Matthew.

Simon looked back to check up on Reuben. Still no progress; he was over in the corner staring at Yehuda. He normally wouldn't care about what Reuben was up to at social events like this, but because he had voiced his concern about being here earlier, he wanted to ensure he was comfortable. Reuben made eye contact with him, and Simon tilted his head towards Matthew and Dan in front of him, suggesting that he participate in the conversation, which Reuben accepted.

'Hi, Reuben. It's been a while,' remarked Matthew. 'How are you?'

'I've been better,' replied Reuben, sighing. 'The food's good, though.'

Matthew laughed.

'Couldn't agree more,' he said.

They then proceeded to the living room, where Asher, Yehuda, Naphtali, Dan, and Matthew played live Jewish music, with Yehuda playing the drums and Dan singing. Somehow, Matthew was able to harmonise with his bass guitar even though he hadn't heard most of the music before. Mr and Mrs Levy, Rachel, Hannah, Simon, and Reuben sat on the sofas, watching.

Hannah sat next to Simon, which made him want to cry. Halfway through the performance, she asked, making him start, 'Hi, what's your name? – Sorry.'

'It's OK. I'm Reuben,' answered Simon, figuring it would be embarrassing to reveal his true identity and thus expose himself to the one who had rejected the prospect of ever dating him.

'And is this your twin brother?' she asked, eyeing Reuben.

'Yes, it is,' answered Simon, grinning.

'And what's your name?' she asked him.

'Reuben,' he muttered, his mouth full of biscuit.

She raised her eyebrows.

Simon didn't know what to do. He didn't know how he could escape from this one. Luckily, Dan announced the next song they were going to perform and Hannah didn't ask them any more questions, instead focusing on Rachel for the rest of the night, before she had to leave.

Then, Simon, Reuben, Naphtali, Asher, and Dan left together. Simon had had a wonderful night. He had even forgotten that he had recently become unemployed, a state that he would have to get accustomed to, but hopefully, not for long. As he walked down the street with his friends, he couldn't believe he had missed the opportunity to get to know Hannah. She had been right there, sitting next to him! Sure, maybe she was going to seminary, but he could've at least introduced himself and demonstrated the best parts of his personality. Maybe he would've made a good impression upon her. Maybe she would've been interested. Maybe they would've formed a bond that would've long remained after she'd started seminary. Maybe she would've stayed.

Now, Hannah of Hendon would have to remember that night she had met the two odd, young men who not only looked alike, but who also had the same name. But he thought, who knows? Maybe he'd bump into her again, perhaps before she went to seminary. Oh, Hannah of Hendon…

Still, he felt ridiculous for having lost such an opportunity. Not meeting her after trying to plan a first date had been a major disappointment, and now there she had been, and he'd avoided her.

The group reached Golders Green Road, where normally they would split up, as Dan's home was in the opposite direction, but he said to Simon, 'May I have a word with you?'

'Sure,' said Simon, as the others went on their way back to the house.

'Do you mind not bringing Reuben anymore to our get-togethers?' asked Dan.

'I beg your pardon?'

'I feel awful telling you this, but it would be my preference and some others' that he not join us.'

'What? Why? Whose preference?'

'Never mind that,' said Dan. 'The point is, Reuben can be kind of a wet blanket. He can be quite negative, he doesn't really talk all that much, and he just doesn't add so much to the fun. Who knows? Maybe this would be good for him, too.'

'Absolutely not,' said Simon. 'I'm not going to exclude Reuben like that.' Perhaps because Reuben was his twin, Simon felt as though he personally were being insulted.

'Please, Simon.'

'No,' asserted Simon. He was not going to exclude his own brother.

Dan stared at him, looking as if he was trying to figure out the best argument in order to have his way.

'I'd really appreciate it if you obliged me.'

'Shan't,' said Simon, shaking his head. 'Sorry.'

Dan now had a rather bitter expression on his face, one that Simon was not used to being the cause of.

'Very well, then.'

They wished each other a good night and returned to their homes.

As Simon walked home alone, he found it funny that neither Yehuda nor Dan had mentioned anything about the siyyum – whether how proud they were, or how sorry they had been to have missed it. They hadn't even said 'Mazal tov'. But by the time he'd reached home, he'd forgotten all about it.

CHAPTER IV

After the siyyum, Simon had such a good time with everyone that he thought it would be a good idea to plan a get-together with all the housemates. He tried to arrange with Reuben, Asher, and Naphtali a time and place for them to meet, and they all settled on a small restaurant in Hendon in the early afternoon that Sunday.

Chaim called and they spoke for the first time since he had left England. Chaim suggested that they start learning a new tractate soon, but Simon hesitated, then confessed that he was now unemployed and wanted to focus on finding a new job. He also thought he wasn't in such a good place mentally to be taking on such a commitment – learning the tractate of Chullin hadn't been easy.

On the morning of the get-together at the restaurant in Hendon, Naphtali rang Simon and apologised, saying that something had come up with his family, though he didn't say what.

Simon said that was OK, but as he walked towards the restaurant, he had an odd feeling he wouldn't be seeing Asher either. He tried not to dwell on it, though, as it made him sad.

When he arrived at the restaurant, he requested a table by the window for 'perhaps three'. Reuben arrived shortly afterwards, and took a seat opposite Simon.

'Where are they?' asked Reuben.

Simon shrugged, trying to mask any disappointment from his face.

When the waiter came, Simon and Reuben said they needed more time to consider their orders. Although Reuben actually hadn't decided yet, Simon thought it would have been appropriate for the three of them to order the food together once Asher arrived, lest their food came out a lot earlier than his.

Reuben volunteered to send Asher a text message to find out when he would be arriving.

After ten minutes of waiting, Reuben sighed after having checked his mobile again. Simon felt bad to keep Reuben waiting, so he signalled to the waiter to come and take their orders.

He looked around and saw a group of three old people looking to be in their seventies and eighties eating at the table against the wall to his left. He presumed everyone who needed to be there in that group were present, unlike the situation at his table.

'I wonder if he's coming,' said Simon.

Reuben shrugged.

'I don't know, but I'm starving. Honestly, it's wrong for them to be doing this to us.'

Simon was accustomed to Reuben complaining, but he took this accusation against their friends seriously.

'How so?'

'You invite them out and one of them cancels on the day, and the other doesn't show up after fifteen minutes – and that's assuming he'll be coming at all.' Reuben checked his wristwatch.

They had finished the sliced bread and olives between them. Barely a trace of olive oil remained in the white bowl that had contained the olives. Simon was starting to feel rather hungry, even after the appetiser. He could hear the other customers' forks and knives clanking as they sliced their steaks, green beans, and salmon. He looked at their dishes, and his stomach rumbled. He placed an order of chips and lemonade for himself and Reuben just to stifle their hunger. A thought arose in his mind that perhaps there was something rather cruel about the way Naphtali and Asher were going about this situation, but he ignored it.

Finally, once they had finished the chips, Simon decided it was time to order their main dishes. They had given Asher enough time. Their dishes were served about fifteen minutes later. Simon had not only an empty feeling inside due to hunger, but also from abandonment, the latter of which his meal could not satisfy. He kept glancing at the doorway, imagining Asher showing up late, out of breath, and apologising for the major delay. Then he finally accepted the likelihood that Asher wasn't coming.

'I wonder why he didn't come,' he said.

Reuben shrugged, then, with his mouth full of beef ribs as he looked down at his food, said, 'I don't know. That's something you should ask him.'

Simon figured there must have been a good reason for Asher not to come. Nonetheless, he decided not to bring it up with him, figuring if it was important, Asher would bring it up first.

CHAPTER V

Sunday marked the first day of the job search. That day and on every subsequent day, Simon would browse through online listings for office jobs, sending his CV to several organisations throughout London. Sometimes he would go for walks in order to clear his mind for a bit. He'd see Aaron occasionally at the synagogue, but he knew better than to speak to him now; Aaron barely smiled when they'd greet each other, and even if he did, it didn't seem to indicate any desire to converse.

During some of his walks, or sometimes when he went to do the shopping, he'd notice a blond-haired young man walking up his street. One day he noticed him entering the house two doors down. Simon had never seen him before; maybe he was a new neighbour, unless he had always lived there and he had just never noticed him until now. He looked to be around the same age as Simon.

Yehuda, Dan and Matthew would visit and have jam sessions with Naphtali and Asher in the living room in the evenings. Simon assumed this was due to the wonderful music they had produced last Saturday night. He would've joined them, but seeing Naphtali playing his acoustic guitar, he figured there was nothing unique he could add. Nonetheless, he enjoyed listening to them while making tea or just relaxing by the dining table in the dining room.

At one point, Simon overheard Yehuda reply to a question of Dan's that Hannah had left for Israel recently. Simon couldn't stop thinking about the night when she'd initiated a conversation with him. She had seemed interested, but he had lost the opportunity.

It was now Friday morning, and Simon was looking at job listings on his laptop at his desk in his bedroom.

The door was open, and Patrick, Simon's six-year-old orange tabby cat, approached and hopped onto the desk. He lay on his side by the laptop, exposing his belly.

Simon petted his head and then his upper back. Patrick stared up at him approvingly.

Then, as Patrick licked his right paw, Simon counted the number of jobs he had applied to that week: fifty.

He was starting to feel a little stressed, but he was still hopeful. He figured he'd take a break – one of the fifty companies was bound to contact him in the next several weeks or so.

He closed his laptop and decided to play his acoustic guitar on his bed, his back against the wall. He improvised, discovering certain harmonic progressions he found pleasant.

Patrick jumped onto the bed and lay beside him, purring. Simon started humming melodies to harmonise with the chords, which Patrick seemed to enjoy all the more. At least Simon had an audience to please.

Simon started thinking about Chanukah, which was his favourite Jewish holiday, even though it was several months away. He came up with lyrics to which he assigned some melodies. Patrick's tail curled as Simon got up to grab some blank sheets of paper and a pen to write down the lyrics and chords. Patrick purred beside him for a while, then fled when Simon started strumming the guitar with more force. In two hours, he composed a Chanukah song he titled 'Candles'.

When Reuben returned home at a quarter after two, he rushed downstairs to share the exciting news with him. He hadn't composed any music since his teen years.

'Let's have a listen,' said Reuben, sitting on the living room sofa.

Simon sat on another sofa, facing him, and he prepared himself as he looked at the sheets of paper he had placed beside him.

He played the first chord and started singing the song. His pitch was a bit off; he hadn't sung much in years, apart from during the liturgical services at synagogue. When he finished, he looked up to see a rather impressed-looking Reuben.

'That was really good,' said Reuben. 'You wrote all that yourself?'

'Today,' said Simon, grinning as his cheeks blushed.

'Today?'

'Er – earlier in the morning,' added Simon; he still hadn't told anyone he'd lost his job.

'Well, it sounds lovely,' said Reuben.

'Thanks,' said Simon. 'What do you think about the idea of me forming a band with the other guys?'

'I think that'd be a great idea,' remarked Reuben.

Simon looked down as he laid his guitar aside.

'What? You don't think so?' asked Reuben.

'I don't know. I've never really played in an ensemble before; I've only ever played by myself. Maybe I could just write songs to sing while I play the guitar.'

'I think it would be great if you formed a band with everyone else,' remarked Reuben. 'Come on, Simon. They're all gifted musicians. You read music at uni, and you're a very talented guitar player. Music's the only thing you've ever been good at – I mean – interested in. I think you should form a band with them.'

Simon thought about his advice. He had been fantasising about forming a band with his other friends for some time now.

'But they've already got another guitar player, Naphtali. What have I got to give?'

'Your songs,' said Reuben. 'Not to mention your guitar skills. Naphtali plays other instruments, too, and he also sings.'

'All right,' acquiesced Simon, 'I think I'll speak to them about it. Thanks, Reuben!'

CHAPTER VI

Dan invited Simon and their friends to hang out and jam at his house on Sunday night. Simon went with his acoustic guitar, knowing that Naphtali might bring his as well, but he figured Naphtali could play another instrument instead, or they could just have two acoustic guitar players. He brought Reuben along as well, as was customary.

Simon knocked on Dan's front door. Dan opened it, and his smile vanished upon seeing Reuben standing beside Simon.

'Welcome,' he said flatly.

'Thank you,' said Simon, pretending not to notice the change in his demeanour.

Everyone else was already there, which must have brought Reuben comfort. Yehuda, Asher, Naphtali, Matthew, and Mr and Mrs Shapiro were all in the kitchen conversing. Simon greeted Dan's parents. Everyone had left their instruments in the living room, and Simon did the same.

Simon noticed there was a new face, a tall, tan young man speaking to Asher, Naphtali and Dan. He recognised him as the same young man he had seen walking alongside Dan through the window during the siyyum. He looked animated, using his hands and arms to express himself. He seemed to captivate the others as they hung on to his each and every word, making them laugh at his many jokes. Simon could sometimes hear what he was saying even while away conversing with someone else. He identified his accent as American.

'We've got some snacks here,' offered Mrs Shapiro. 'There's also cottage pie and chips if you'd like.'

'Oh, no thanks; I've already eaten,' replied Reuben.

Dan stared at Reuben disappointedly.

Reuben continued to stand by the counter with his arms crossed.

Simon turned to Yehuda.

'Who's that?' he asked, looking at the stranger.

'That's Adam Becker. He's a friend of Dan's. Dan invited him since he's also into music.'

'Oh, fantastic,' said Simon. 'I was wondering, what do you think about the idea of us forming a band, as in, to actually make our own music and perform for others?'

'I'd love that,' said Yehuda. 'That's an excellent idea. I'd like to know what the others think about it, too.'

Simon was pleased that Yehuda was on board. He headed towards Adam, overhearing Reuben complaining about his job to Mr Shapiro along the way. Adam looked up at him as he approached, and Asher, Napthali and Dan all turned towards him too.

They introduced themselves to each other.

'Are you from America?' asked Simon.

'Originally, yes,' answered Adam. 'I grew up in LA. I moved here just before starting secondary school.'

It turned out that Adam had gone to a different Jewish secondary school from everyone else and had met Dan through a mutual friend.

'I hear you're musical. What instrument do you play?' asked Simon.

'The guitar,' replied Adam. 'And you?'

Simon stuttered, 'I also do.'

'Ah, we'll have to see you play, then,' said Adam.

Adam proceeded to talk about his career ambitions of one day owning a company. Later, they all played music together in the living room, mostly improvising, before having a few drinks and chatting.

At the end of the evening, Simon left with Reuben, Asher, and Naphtali so they could go home together.

'Thanks so much,' Simon said to Dan, as the other three went out ahead of him.

'Can I talk to you for a second?' asked Dan, his expression serious.

'Sure,' replied Simon, as the other three kept walking.

'Would you please not invite Reuben next time?' Dan asked.

'No –'

'I invited you and you brought him and it's my house.'

Simon nodded; it was true.

'Right. I'm sorry, but –'

'I'm not the only one who feels this way; others have told me about it, too. He just looks like he's never enjoying being with us. It's weird and no fun. We'd just prefer that you not bring him along anymore. We're friends with *you*. That's how it's always been until you moved into his house. Please respect this.'

Simon sighed.
'Fine.'

CHAPTER VII

Dan brought Adam along to all of the subsequent get-togethers that Simon's friends planned. Simon couldn't help but notice that everyone seemed to be growing fonder of Adam. One Wednesday night, Yehuda invited everyone over to his house. They all were standing around in the kitchen drinking beer.

Somehow, the conversation centred on Adam throughout most of the night, whether it concerned his traits or things he was up to. Simon was starting to wonder whether anyone else in the group mattered enough to be asked a question. Adam would joke around with them, and there came a point where everyone started praising him, and they appeared to be going around in a circle, with Simon in front of Adam, thus halfway through the crescent of compliments.

'You're so funny, isn't he so funny?' started Yehuda, pointing at Adam, standing next to him, his bottle of beer in his hand as he grinned at everyone else. He probably hadn't intended to start the cycle.

'Yes, very funny, and good-looking as well!' added Dan.

'And smart,' said Matthew.

Next up was Simon, apparently, and everyone looked at him, obviously expecting him to say something positive about Adam, who was smirking before him, but Simon only smiled and nodded. He was feeling a bit dazed from all the beer he had drunk. He had met Adam very recently, and he didn't know him well nor had he spent much time getting to know him. He was sure he had many positive qualities, but he felt as though any compliment he could offer would feel insincere. He also thought it was rather odd that the others were engaging in such behaviour.

What he hadn't necessarily intended, which was what ended up happening, was to stop the current of praise. Next to him, Asher, who must have been waiting for Simon to speak, didn't continue the pattern out of confusion.

During that brief moment of silence, Simon saw that Adam was scowling at him, which paralysed him. He had never meant to insult him. He didn't think poorly of Adam, he just didn't think much of him to begin with due to his ignorance. Perhaps the others had been able to get to know him better.

Before he knew it, Adam was smiling again and engaging in conversation with everyone else. Simon was a bit taken aback. He wondered if he had been the only one who had noticed Adam's sudden change in facial expression. He was starting to doubt whether it had actually happened. Or maybe he had misread him.

Either way, the conversation continued. They kept talking about Adam and his life throughout most of the rest of the conversation that night. Even though Simon ended up enjoying himself overall, the face that Adam had made troubled him. He thought about asking someone about it, but now wasn't the time. He wondered whom he could ask later, but thought maybe it was best not to, so as not to speak poorly against him.

Nonetheless, upon his return home, he remembered that he had intended to bring up the subject of starting a band with his friends. He hadn't had the chance since everyone had kept talking about Adam the whole time. He wondered when he would have the opportunity to do so.

CHAPTER VIII

The next morning, Simon woke up with an excruciating headache. He had a fever, with aches throughout his body and a sore throat, fatigue, and a cough. He had come down with the flu.

He couldn't get out of bed until past ten o'clock. He felt terrible that he'd missed the morning service at synagogue, and even though he was too ill to pray at synagogue, it was past the time to say the morning Shema, which contained passages of the Bible he was required to recite every morning and evening, and by the time he managed to wash his hands, brush his teeth, and sluggishly shower himself, it was past the time to pray the Shemoneh Esreh prayer too, a prayer he was required to recite three times every day and by a certain time.

Although he was full of guilt after not having recited these parts of the morning service and pain from his illness, he pushed himself to don phylacteries, which took him much longer than usual.

Once he was finished, he put his phylacteries away and asked God to make him feel better. He sighed and sat on his bed, his eyes barely able to stay open for more than a few seconds. It was past eleven o'clock and all he wanted to do was sleep. It was like the first morning of Shavuot, the first night of which holiday he'd customarily stay up spending most of the time learning Torah.

The entire house was empty and quiet as everyone was out working, which made it a much more accommodating environment to sleep in.

He closed the blind of his window to darken the bedroom. As he did so, he remembered that it was Yehuda's birthday today, and all his friends were going to his house tonight to celebrate. He felt terrible that he'd have to miss one of his closest friend's birthday parties. He had even bought beer for him and his friends, which he had stored in the refrigerator downstairs.

He thought about how he had become ill. Who had exhibited symptoms of the flu recently? Everyone had been fine yesterday at Yehuda's house.

He then remembered when he had been doing the shopping at the local kosher supermarket yesterday there had been a person with a terrible cough standing near him by the refrigerators. He had managed to scuttle off, but the same man had later stood behind him while queuing, and continued his series of coughs, and Simon hadn't been able to edge closer ahead without intruding into the personal space of the shopper before him. Even though he hadn't wanted to make the man feel bad by switching queues, it would have been too inconvenient anyway as the other queues had had several people waiting in them at the time. It hadn't helped that the woman in front of him had unloaded enough food to feed a whole yeshiva onto the conveyor belt. He had stood around for so long while exposed to this man's cough, he had almost been destined to catch the flu. But, there was nothing he could do about it now, as sad as he was. He sent Yehuda a text message telling him he was ill and sad not to be able to attend the party. Minutes after putting his mobile down onto the bed beside him, he effortlessly fell asleep.

When Simon woke up, his bedroom was so dark due to the closed shade that he couldn't guess what time it was. He felt around him and came into contact with his mobile, which indicated it was seven in the evening. Although he had a bit more stamina now, he still felt relentlessly lethargic.

He went downstairs to make himself some soup. No one was home, so he didn't have to worry about infecting anyone while outside of his bedroom. He made sure to clean any surfaces he touched. He felt a bit low knowing that he was probably missing Yehuda's birthday party right now.

Funnily enough, he thought, Yehuda hadn't responded to his text message. He figured he was busy preparing for or celebrating his birthday and thus was too busy to respond. Simon would have to prepare meals for himself for Shabbat as he had no sign of getting better any time soon, and he didn't want to infect his parents or any of his housemates, wherever they were going for the meals. Although he would have normally done the shopping for Shabbat in such a case, he had such a minimal appetite, he felt it wasn't necessary; he'd just use the ingredients he already had. He would ask Reuben to buy him some small rolls of challah the next day. They had extra wine at home.

Simon carried the bowl of soup upstairs to his bedroom. No one came home while he ate it. He forced himself to stay awake after finishing his soup, long enough to take the empty bowl to the kitchen sink downstairs, after which he returned to his bed upstairs and fell asleep again.

The next day was Friday, and Simon felt even more fatigued than the day before, which he hadn't thought possible. He prepared some simple appetisers hours before Shabbat started; he hadn't been able to ask Reuben to purchase some challah for him as he had been asleep. He ended up using some matzah they had stored in a cupboard for bread. When Shabbat started, he prayed the afternoon and evening prayers in his quiet house. He had no idea where his housemates were. He felt bad as he had forgotten to light candles for the Sabbath.

Simon briefly woke up that night to the sound of Asher and Naphtali's laughter as they arrived home from wherever they had gone for dinner. He felt sad, as if he had been missing out. He had missed Yehuda's birthday the previous night and wherever Asher and Naphtali could have been tonight. He wanted to go downstairs and talk to them, but even if he had the energy to do so, he couldn't go near them and possibly infect them, so he remained isolated in his dark bedroom. He fell asleep within minutes after having been awoken. The next morning, he prayed that Hashem healed him and improved his life, including finding meaningful work, though upon second thought, he wasn't sure if this were the best thing to pray for during the day of rest, when one ideally shouldn't speak about business.

After a peaceful, sleepy Shabbat, Simon was starting to feel markedly better by Sunday, though he still had a bit of a lingering headache and cough.

By the evening, he was starting to feel almost normal, and he encountered Naphtali in the kitchen when he went to make himself a cup of tea.

'Oh, Simon. I haven't seen you in a while,' said Naphtali, who was boiling rice and pasta.

'Yeah, I was ill, but I do feel a lot better now,' said Simon, making sure not to stand too close.

'Ah, great,' said Naphtali. Simon thought about the last time he had got together with his friends. It had been on Wednesday, when they had been at Yehuda's house. He remembered that foul look Adam had given him, which made him shiver to think about as he grabbed the handle of the electric kettle, which had just finished boiling.

'Naphtali, what do you think about Adam?' he asked.

Naphtali shrugged.

'Seems nice. You?'

Simon paused before expressing his thoughts.

'I don't know. He just sort of rubs me up the wrong way. It's a bit hard to explain.'

'How so?' enquired Naphtali, looking confused as he stirred the pasta in the large pot, the sound of the boiling water filling the air.

Simon paused again. 'I just remember that time we were together in Yehuda's house. I'm not sure if it's because I didn't give him any compliments, but he sort of gave me a strange look.'

'Oh, Simon,' said Naphtali dismissively, 'you're being too sensitive.'

'About what?' asked Asher, entering the kitchen behind them.

'Nothing,' said Simon, just as Naphtali said, 'About Adam.'

'What about him?' continued Asher.

'It's nothing,' assured Simon, not wanting to make his sentiments public.

He thought it best not to bring it up anymore.

CHAPTER IX

Rabbi Isaacs announced the beginning of a new class that he would start teaching every Tuesday night on Rashi's commentary on the weekly parsha. Simon attended the first class and thoroughly enjoyed it. It was also a nice escape from the stress he felt regarding not having a job. There were five attendees, including him and the new guy he had noticed living just down the street. He meant to introduce himself, but by the time he had thanked Rabbi Isaacs for the wonderful lesson, he had gone.

Throughout the rest of that week, he spent his time learning more Torah, including Rashi's commentary on the parsha. He also had more time to tend the garden. He wrote a new song called 'The New Year' as Rosh Hashanah was drawing close.

He didn't show it to anyone; he still wanted to refine it. He found it delightful that he had more time for music. He found all these activities very fulfilling.

That Shabbat, the neighbour he had recently noticed for the first time attended services at his synagogue, and so Simon decided to approach him and welcome him during kiddush Saturday morning.

'Are you new to the area?' asked Simon.

'No,' answered the young man, whose name turned out to be Ezra Cohen. 'I grew up in Golders Green, but I've just recently moved back after studying in Israel for a few years.'

'I've seen you in the class that Rabbi Isaacs gives on Rashi. How have you been enjoying it so far?'

'Very much so,' answered Ezra. 'I'd like to learn more if I could. I've actually been trying to lately.'

'So have I,' said Simon.

'Why don't we learn it together?' suggested Ezra.

'I'd love to. When are you free?' asked Simon, suddenly remembering that it was he who abruptly had much more spare time.

'How about Mondays, how would that work?'

'That works. Feel free to bring any friends,' said Simon.

So, they came up with Tea and Torah, a weekly programme on Monday nights at Simon's house, featuring learning Rashi's commentary on the weekly parsha, and Simon and Ezra's friends were welcome to join if they wanted. After Shabbat ended, Simon notified his friends on the new weekly event.

Monday night came, and Simon bought refreshments and laid them out on the dining table, where he, Ezra, and whoever else desired to attend would be learning together. He then decided to prepare tea, suddenly remembering that he had to prepare the very beverage the event was named after. He served four cups of tea and sat down, the steam rising from the white mugs as he wondered how many people would actually show up.

The doorbell rang. He jumped and got up and found that it was Ezra. They waited a few minutes. Simon gave him a cup of tea.

'How are you?' asked Simon after they sat down by the dining table, the book of Rashi's commentary lying in front of them.

'Thank God,' said Ezra, 'very well. Everything Hashem does is for the best, whether we realise it or not.'

They then decided to start. A few minutes in, Asher and Yehuda came.

'I heard you guys are learning Rashi,' said Yehuda.

'You're welcome to join,' said Simon.

'Don't mind if I do,' said Yehuda.

So, Asher and Yehuda hung their raincoats on the coat rack on the wall and joined them, helping themselves to a cup of tea and some biscuits. Simon wondered whether he would have to make a fifth cup of tea. He was glad that some of his friends were attending, even if it didn't appear to be predetermined.

The session lasted about an hour. Reuben floated in and out of the dining room in his pyjamas a couple of times before giving in to Simon's invitations and joining in the last ten minutes of the session before they called it a night. Simon made Reuben a cup of tea before they finished the first learning session.

'Did you know that we're starting a band?' Yehuda asked Simon.

'No.'

Yehuda nodded excitedly.

'Yeah. We are. Adam's trying to organise it.'

Simon was taken aback. It had been his idea to form a band with his friends, and more just for fun. It seemed like they were trying to pursue some serious endeavour.

Reuben eyed Simon expectantly.

Simon knew Reuben wanted him to invite himself to join the new group, but Simon was still unaware of all the details. But he didn't have to enquire, because Yehuda went on, 'So far, it's me, Asher, and we're trying to get Matthew, Naphtali and Dan to join too.'

Simon wanted to ask whether he could join, but he felt a bit odd doing so. They knew he could play guitar; their love of music had been one of the things that had bonded them in school. Why hadn't any of them asked him?

'May I join?' he finally asked.

A surprising silence filled the room, one that lasted several seconds that stretched endlessly in Simon's mind. He felt awful.

'You'd have to ask Adam,' said Yehuda finally.

Simon, taken aback by the sudden worried looks on Asher and Yehuda's faces, said, 'OK.'

Simon was surprised. Less than two weeks ago, they had all jammed together and he had suggested forming a band to Yehuda. Now, Adam was doing that very thing, and the originator of the idea wasn't being included?

Yehuda and Asher got up and left, and then Ezra thanked Simon for his time and for hosting him. Simon introduced him to Reuben, and they escorted him to the door. On his way out, he turned to Simon and asked, 'By the way, how is the job search going?'

Simon froze.

'What?' asked Reuben, standing behind him.

'Er, not so well,' replied Simon.

Ezra saw that there was shock on Reuben's face. He looked at Simon. 'Oh, I'm so sorry. Was I not supposed to –'

'No, that's fine,' said Simon, waving his hand.

'You're looking for a job?' asked Reuben.

'OK. See you later,' said Simon, holding the door open as Ezra exited.

'OK, see you. Goodnight,' Ezra said awkwardly as he departed.

Simon closed the door, left with a puzzled-looking Reuben.

'You're looking for a job?' he asked again.

Simon sighed.

'Yes.'

'Since when?'

'About two weeks now.'

'Why? You don't like your job?'

'I haven't got one.'

Reuben's jaw hung.

'Why didn't you tell me?'

'Because I didn't want to worry you,' explained Simon. 'Besides, it's embarrassing enough. I'm trying to find one.'

'I hope you find one soon,' said Reuben, though Simon couldn't tell whether this was more out of goodwill or insecurity.

Either way, he would pause applying for jobs. Rosh Hashanah was four days away. He wanted to give the fifty or so companies he had applied to a chance to review his applications. Also, with the High Holidays and Succot coming, he wasn't sure if asking for several days off shortly after commencing a job would give a very good impression.

CHAPTER X

Later that week, Simon overheard Naphtali telling Asher in the kitchen that he had been accepted into the band, which apparently was called 'The Beis', homophonous with the word 'bass'. He felt a bit intimidated, as if time was running out to be a part of the band, but there was no sign of them no longer accepting new members, and they were all supposed to meet Sunday night at Dan's house, which was Motzei Rosh Hashanah. Either way, he belonged to the group, so he was sure to be considered.

Rosh Hashanah arrived, and Simon thought about the misfortune that had come about towards the end of the Jewish year, namely the termination of his job and the lost opportunity with Hannah. He hoped that the new year would bring meaningful work, success, and inner peace. He prayed for all these things during the prayer services throughout Rosh Hashanah at synagogue and privately at home. Simon and Reuben spent all the meals at their parents' house.

On Sunday night, Simon and his friends headed to Dan's house. There, Mr and Mrs Shapiro hosted them. They were enjoying themselves and preparing for the Fast of Gedalia, which was the next day. Simon made sure to consume a lot of chicken, beef, and rice, as well as loads of water.

Simon took this as an opportunity to ask Adam whether he could join the band. Towards dessert, he went to his corner of the table.

'I hear I need to ask you to audition if I'd like to be in the band,' said Simon.

'Yes, well, I'm the manager, so, yes,' replied Adam.

The band is already a brand? thought Simon.

'So, when would be a good time?' he asked, assuming he was already entitled to a try.

'Well, I'm going to be a bit busy now,' said Adam, 'so, I would suggest at some point after Yom Kippur.' He looked down at his slice of cake, slicing a piece and eating it.

'OK,' said Simon. Seeing that Adam seemed more interested in finishing his slice of cake than continuing the conversation, he returned to his seat.

Everyone else seemed to be really amusing themselves. The table was filled with laughter and comments about a good future involving the theoretical band, rehearsals and performances. Though Simon appreciated these positive remarks and wished every success life had to give his friends, he had the strange feeling that he was being left out. A part of him refused to believe that his whole group of friends from secondary school could – or at least would – do such a thing, so he didn't think so much about it. At around half past ten, he figured he'd had enough and decided to walk home alone.

After walking through the streets, he entered the house and was a bit surprised to see Reuben come downstairs in his pyjamas within seconds.

'Where were you?' asked Reuben.

Simon froze. Had he missed some event Reuben had invited him to?

'Er, I was at Dan's.'

'Yeah, I know, cos I heard the others talking about it. Why didn't you tell me you were going there?'

Simon paused again.

'Was I supposed to?' he asked eventually.

'Yes, you were.' Reuben nodded enthusiastically in agreement with himself. 'How else was I supposed to know when to get ready and leave?'

'You weren't invited,' said Simon, a bit surprised at how bluntly the words had come out of his mouth.

Reuben gasped.

'What?'

'You weren't invited, were you? Did they actually invite you?'

'No, but I always join you guys.'

Simon struggled with what to say next, but he figured the only way to put it was directly and clearly. 'They don't want you to come to the get-togethers.'

Reuben's jaw dropped.

'What?' he said again.

'They don't want you to hang out with them. That's what I've been told. That's not my preference, Reuben. It's theirs.'

'Since when?'

'That I can't tell you, sorry.'

'But what do I do?' said Reuben, wincing.

Simon shrugged.

'I don't know. Why don't you hang out with your friends?'

'But Simon, your friends *are* my friends.'

'No, they're not,' said Simon, now questioning his own response.

'Yes, they are,' replied Reuben.

'How so? What about your friends from yeshiva?'

'That was then,' said Reuben. 'Yes, I had friends in yeshiva, yes, but then I got to know your friends after spending time with them here, and they're much better friends. The friends I had in yeshiva were not very nice. But whatever, it doesn't matter anymore because they don't want to hang out with me. Fine.'

Reuben turned around and headed up the stairs and into his room.

Simon stood by the door, staring ahead as his ears rang in the silence, still processing the encounter he had just had. It had been his responsibility to tell Reuben before now, but it had been too painful, so he had avoided the conversation. He figured that Reuben would come to understand eventually. It had obviously come as a shock to him, which Simon hadn't intended. At least he could now deal with the truth of the situation, he thought.

CHAPTER XI

Adam must have forgotten about the audition, thought Simon, because Yom Kippur had passed, and he knew that everyone would be too busy during Succot to plan an audition, so he decided to take advantage before Succot came and rang Adam, reminding him about the audition. Adam suggested meeting him, Dan and Yehuda at Dan's house that night, and Simon agreed. Seeing that it was a same-day notice, he barely had a chance to practise.

He carried his guitar to Dan's house that night, where he met Adam, Dan and Yehuda.

'Which instrument do you play?' asked Adam as they stood in the dining room, his arms crossed.

'I play the acoustic guitar,' answered Simon.

'Humph,' uttered Adam. 'Let's go over here.'

Adam led them to the living room. This was where they had played the other night when they had all been there jamming, but now Dan, Adam and Yehuda sat there on the sofa before him, with Adam in the centre.

Mr and Mrs Shapiro passed by on their way to the kitchen as Simon withdrew his guitar from its case with shaky hands.

'Oh, are you going to audition now?' observed Mrs Shapiro. 'Can we watch?'

Simon would have preferred it if they hadn't; having three judges staring at him was enough to make him anxious, but he couldn't refuse, not only because he was too submissive, but because if he wanted to prove himself as a potentially good member of the band, he had to show that he was capable of performing in front of others. Besides, he would also be showcasing original material.

'Sure,' he answered. He looked at the judges and said, 'The first song I'm going to play is a song I wrote called "Candles".'

Simon's plan was to put his best foot forward, playing the more developed of his two songs before performing others. This would also demonstrate his capability to compose original music, which was essential for the band.

He started playing the song, and the notes were coming out correctly as he strummed and sang. He caught a glimpse of Mr and Mrs Shapiro. They were grinning. He looked again at the judges during the first repetition of the chorus, but their faces told a different story. Dan looked indifferent, maybe even a little upset to be here. Adam's expression was flat, and Yehuda looked like he was trying to follow a mathematical equation.

He finished, and waited.

Mr and Mrs Shapiro clapped, but quickly stopped as Yehuda started sharing his feedback.

'It's a nice song,' commented Yehuda, 'but I think it needs a little more work. I do enjoy your singing and guitar playing.'

'Thank you,' said Simon, nodding and feeling as though he were on *The X Factor*.

He looked at Adam, who was sitting next to Yehuda, but Dan spoke next.

'Not bad,' he said.

'Is there anything else you can play?' asked Adam.

'Why don't you play some Jewish music, something we'd all know the sound of?' suggested Yehuda.

'All right,' said Simon, scrapping his plan to play his song 'The New Year' next.

He played some Shabbat zemirot, and there were two distinct instances in which he made a mistake. He'd pause before repeating the chords with trembling hands and knees. There was a point when he looked up and saw Adam staring at him with an intense, almost dark stare. He was a bit taken aback by this, but he was almost finished with the third Shabbat song, and then stopped.

'That was pretty good,' said Dan.

Yehuda nodded.

'Not bad,' said Yehuda.

'Thank you,' said Adam. 'We'll talk about it and let you know what we think.'

Simon was taken aback. He almost felt entitled to being a part of the band; it had been his idea and they were his friends.

Mr and Mrs Shapiro clapped again.

'Well done,' said Mrs Shapiro.

'That was great,' said Mr Shapiro.

But due to the serious looks now settling on the judges' faces, they finally scuttled off.

Simon wondered whether they had been this serious when the others had auditioned for the band. He wanted to ask them when he'd find out whether he'd be accepted, but he didn't want to come across as desperate or too pushy.

'Thank you,' he said.

They then chatted for a bit, and then Simon decided he would've liked to go home. He bade them goodbye, and Adam approached him.

'Hey, could we take a short walk?' Adam asked him. 'I could walk you home.'

'Sure,' answered Simon as he grabbed his guitar case. As long as that was where he'd end up, he didn't mind. Still, he found Adam's approach a bit abrupt.

So, they left Dan's house and walked outside together. Simon worried he was trying to reject him gracefully. He would've much rather got a 'No' now than receive the bad news ten minutes later upon arriving home.

'I'd like to know,' began Adam in a softer than usual tone, as if to indicate trust, 'what do you think of the others' skills?'

'Just the rest of the band?' asked Simon.

'Yeah.'

Simon thought about it. He had never seriously critiqued his friends' musicianship, instead only forming a general opinion of their sound.

'I think Matthew plays the bass guitar great. Dan's a really good singer. Asher's good on the electric guitar, though I think Yehuda could use a little more practice on the drums. I think sometimes he isn't in the same rhythm as the rest of us. Other than that, they're great. I think Dan could work on his pitch a bit more.'

Adam nodded.

'OK,' he said.

They reached Simon's house and stopped in front of it. A part of Simon felt weird that he was exposing to Adam where he lived.

'Well, thank you for walking me home,' he said, not really wanting to invite him in.

'You're very welcome. Have a good night,' said Adam, waving and turning around.

'You as well,' said Simon.

He then helped Reuben build a succah in the garden.

CHAPTER XII

Succot was approaching. As Simon had so much time on his hands, he started preparing meals on Wednesday night (Succot would commence with Shabbat this year). He was planning to invite his close friends for a meal on the second day of Succot for lunch. He sent out the invitations by text message. He would host everyone in the succah that he and Reuben had built. To his surprise, Asher and Naphtali had not helped, though due to all the time Simon had, it had still only taken two days to build.

After doing the shopping, Simon came home to find Reuben had left dirty dishes on the dining room table and in the sink. He sighed and cleaned up; he needed the space for cooking.

Reuben appeared a few minutes later.

As Simon was washing a plate Reuben had left on the dining table, he called out to him, 'You left your dirty cups and plates around.'

'Sorry,' said Reuben.

Simon shook his head.

'You've been doing this a lot lately,' he yelled. 'Could you be a bit more mindful?'

Reuben narrowed his eyes and bit his lip. 'Sure.'

Simon still hadn't received any updates regarding the outcome of his audition. He wondered whether anyone would share any insights during the upcoming holidays. Maybe Dan or Yehuda would give some hints as to what the decision would be as they had been judges. This wasn't the reason he hadn't invited Adam, however; he just wanted to spend quality time with people he'd known longer, with the exception of Ezra, whom he had already grown fond of.

By Thursday, everyone had accepted the invitation except Dan, who had declined without giving any reason, and Yehuda, who hadn't responded. Simon called him, but it went to voicemail. He left him a message and assumed he might come, so he prepared enough food for seven people. If he didn't come, there would just be extra food.

Friday came, and as Reuben was out working, it was up to Simon to finish the meals by himself. He noticed that the pillows that Reuben had knocked to the floor after lying on the sofa last night were still scattered around the living room. So, once someone came home and he saw it was him, he admonished him, saying 'You left the pillows on the floor in the living room. I'm tired of cleaning up after your mess. You're really starting to irritate me.'

'I'm sorry,' said Reuben, sounding as though he were about to sob.

Simon sighed as he completed the final steps of the food preparations. Reuben kept apologising, but his behaviour wouldn't change.

Simon and Reuben spent the first three meals at their parents' succah. Once Simon and Reuben arrived from synagogue on Sunday after the morning service, they immediately began setting up the meal for all the guests. Simon's heart was racing; he had never hosted so many people for a holiday meal before; maybe now wasn't the best time to start, he thought.

He enjoyed the silence and emptiness of the house while it lasted; he still had time to set up before his guests arrived. He picked up a large, heavy pot filled with rice from the blech over the stove. He turned around to leave the kitchen when somehow, as he held it with oven mittens, it slipped from his hands and fell to the floor. A hill of rice lay before him as the lid of the pot rolled like a loose tyre, coming to a stop under the dining table in front of him.

'What happened?' called Reuben, who entered the scene and gasped. He helped Simon clean up the mess. Simon saw that there was still some rice left in the pot, but not enough to bother serving seven people.

'Thanks,' said Simon. 'Could you just take everything else to the succah? I'll take it from here.'

'Sure,' said Reuben. He grabbed the tray of Jerusalem kugel and disappeared. 'Er, Simon,' he said, his tone filled with fear.

Simon grew anxious. What was wrong now?

'Come and look,' called Reuben from the living room.

Simon dried his hands with a hand towel and approached. He saw Reuben by the back door, staring out into the garden.

Before reaching near him, he already saw what it was: the succah that he and Reuben had built had been reduced to a pile of rubble in the garden. It had rained a lot, and it had been very windy; the succah had been too vulnerable and the gusts had blown it down at some point.

As if losing a dish of rice had been the worst of his problems, thought Simon. Now he wasn't sure where the meal was going to take place.

'There's still Mum and Dad's succah,' said Reuben, as if he were reading his mind. 'We could just take the food there.'

'Yeah, but they should be eating any time soon, too. There isn't so much space in there; it was built for four people, not eleven,' said Simon, sighing. 'I can't believe this.'

Simon started as someone knocked on the front door.

Reuben went to answer it.

'I'll ask them if they'd mind if we eat there,' said Simon.

He grabbed a pot of chicken in the kitchen; there was no doubt he'd be eating in his parents' succah; he might as well start carrying the food there. Where else were they going to eat?

Reuben opened the door. Asher and Ezra were there.

'Hey,' said Ezra, grinning.

'I'm sorry, but there's been a major accident,' announced Simon, and suddenly, both of their faces were full of fear. 'The succah has collapsed, so I'm going to ask my parents whether we could go eat there.'

Ezra nodded. 'OK. Do you need help carrying the food there?' he asked.

'That would be very helpful,' said Simon. 'Reuben, can you show Ezra where the food is?'

'Sure,' replied Reuben, leading him inside.

'Where's Naphtali?' asked Simon.

'He went to eat with Adam and his family,' said Asher.

'Oh, OK,' said Simon, recalling that he had accepted his invitation. 'And what about Yehuda? Do you know if he's coming?'

'He's also at Adam's,' said Asher sombrely, almost sounding as if he would have preferred to join them, too.

Ezra emerged with the tray of beef.

'I'll stay here in case Matthew comes; that way, he'll know about the situation,' said Reuben.

'OK, thanks,' said Simon, and left with Ezra.

'Thank you so much for your help,' he said as he and Ezra carried the food down Golders Green Road.

'You're very welcome,' replied Ezra.

They caught sight of Matthew coming towards them.

'I hope I'm not late,' he said.

'No, not at all,' said Simon. 'The succah fell, so I'm going to ask my parents if we could all eat at theirs.'

'Oh, OK,' said Matthew, looking utterly confused.

'The succah is that hut I was telling you about,' Simon reminded him.

'Oh, right,' said Matthew, not understanding the gravity of what the succah's collapse entailed. All meals that included bread during Succot had to take place in a succah. 'Well, can I help you?'

'No, that's fine, thanks,' said Simon. 'I don't want to pressure my parents. Do you mind going to my house and I'll meet you there and let you know what they say? That way we could all just bring over the remaining food.'

'Not at all,' said Matthew.

'By the way, any word on the audition?' asked Simon.

Matthew shrugged.

'I don't know. Sorry.'

'That's all right.'

'I hope you get in,' said Matthew, an earnest look on his face.

'Thank you,' said Simon. 'I'll see you soon.'

As Simon and Ezra continued walking, Simon remembered when Ezra had mentioned during their first learning session about everything that God sent his way being for the best. He couldn't see how this could be for the best. Here he was, trying to observe His will by eating in a succah and by giving to his friends, and it felt as though he were being seriously punished.

Simon and Ezra completed their first trip. Simon's parents lived ten minutes away from him on foot. He knocked on the front door. He hoped that someone would be inside to hear them. If they were already in the succah in their garden, they wouldn't be able to hear.

Mrs Jacobs opened the door.

'Hi, Mum.'

'Simon, what are you doing here? I thought you'd be eating in your succah.'

'That was what I had intended, but the succah has blown down.'

Mr Jacobs emerged from the shadowy interior of the house, his eyes filled with fear as he saw Simon and some stranger to him carrying food outside.

Simon wished that he hadn't needed to share the unfortunate news about the succah. His parents were easily prone to anxiety, and such an event, though largely due to the fierce storm, a factor inherently out of his control, would've probably made them wish for him and Reuben to never attempt to build another succah ever again, but he would have to raise his own family, he would've pleaded.

'May we eat in your succah? I've cooked food,' said Simon.

Mrs Jacobs was quiet as she took in all the details of the situation.

She drew in a deep breath and said, 'Yes, but there isn't so much space.'

'Great, I'll just leave this and go get everyone else,' said Simon as he was about to enter the house.

'Everyone else?' said Mrs Jacobs, as both of his bespectacled parents looked at him with anxious expressions.

'Well, yeah, there's about five of us,' said Simon.

'That would be difficult,' said Mrs Jacobs, working out the logistics in her head. 'I would say that four more would be difficult.'

Simon sighed.

'Maybe – I don't know. I'll go and tell the others.'

So, Simon left the tray of chicken on his parents' dining table and rushed back to his house, not realising he had left Ezra behind.

He arrived home and found the front door open. Reuben and Matthew were chatting casually on the living room sofas.

'Where's Asher?' asked Simon.

'Oh, he said he'd rather just eat with his parents in their succah.'

Simon couldn't believe it. Sure, this would make it easier for his parents, but he had agreed to eat with him. He didn't even want to think about how upset he was that everyone else hadn't come, as he wanted to remain joyous in the spirit of the holiday.

'OK, well, that's good, because Mum and Dad said they could take four more people.'

'But we're three,' said Reuben.

'Ezra's there,' Simon reminded him.

So, the three of them were able to bring the rest of the food over. They all somehow managed to crowd together in the small succah.

CHAPTER XIII

Throughout Chol Hamoed, or the intermediate days of Succot, Simon didn't receive a response from Adam as to whether he had been accepted into the band or not. He figured he would just ask him after Simchat Torah. However, he couldn't help but remember how quickly everyone else had become members of the band. Why was it taking so long for him to receive a response?

He and Reuben ate the meals of Shemini Atzeret at their parents' house, as well as the meals of Simchat Torah. However, during his attendance at synagogue on Shemini Atzeret, he heard murmurs from the congregants about a terrorist attack and felt uneasy. He focused on the words of the prayers, even though he couldn't understand some of them as they were in Hebrew. People later laughed and exchanged jokes, and he was getting into the holiday spirit again.

That night, he and his fellow congregants danced on the streets with Torah scrolls for Simchat Torah. There was so much joy as everyone danced and jumped around.

Simon spotted Ezra in the crowd.

'Gut Yom Tov!' he said.

'Guv Tom Tov,' said Ezra.

'Have you heard the news? I've been hearing about some sort of a terrorist attack, but I don't know so much about it,' said Simon.

'There's been an attack in Israel,' answered Ezra. 'Some say it's Hamas. I don't know too many details about it, either.'

Simon froze as Ezra jumped, dancing.

'What? Where? Has anyone been hurt?' asked Simon, immediately thinking of his friend, Chaim, who lived in Jerusalem.

Ezra shrugged.

'I don't know. Some say in the south, rockets everywhere,' he said, casually, but he didn't stop jumping. 'But we must be happy now! We must be b'simcha!' he said, which meant to be with joy.

Simon couldn't bring himself to mirror his movements. He wanted to ask him whether he knew of anyone in Israel. It truly felt like the end of the world.

'I forgot to tell you, but I'll be going on holiday next week,' said Ezra. 'I'll be going to visit some relatives in Australia for a couple of weeks.'

'Oh, so, you and Rabbi Isaacs will be gone,' noticed Simon, as Rabbi Isaacs had announced that he would be visiting his wife's family soon in Canada.

Simon somehow brought himself to dance, which was made easier as that was what everyone else was doing that night. Ignorance was surely not his bliss however. He would spend the remaining services of Simchat Torah praying with the people of Israel in mind. He could think of nothing else, and he could listen to no more rumours as it would only fill him with more anxiety.

Once Simchat Torah had ended and he was able to use his mobile again, he called Chaim, but there was no answer. He figured that Chaim was probably being bombarded with calls. He would try again the next day. For the second night in a row, he would lose several hours of sleep.

The next day, after the morning service at synagogue, he called Chaim again. Still, there was no response. Although he might normally have panicked in this scenario, he had learnt some more about the attack now and knew that most of the casualties had been in the south and that reassured him that at least Chaim should be OK.

After breakfast, he called Adam to ask whether he was part of the band or not, but Adam didn't respond either. He wondered whether it was International Missed Call Day.

There was no one else in the house right now. It was a regular Monday; everyone else was out working. Patrick was probably upstairs napping on his bed.

He decided to go for a walk to take his mind off things.

It was overcast, and the air was getting a bit cooler. He strolled down Golders Green Road and approached a newsstand. He looked at it casually, when the image of a peculiarly familiar face appearing on the top of one of the stacks of newspapers caught his eye. He drew closer and saw that it was the most recent issue of *The Guardian*, and the headline featured the hundreds of hostages that had been taken by Hamas terrorists, and one of the two faces on the front page was of 'Chaim Spiegel, 25'.

Simon's hands trembled as he picked up the newspaper. His friend had been taken hostage. He had to browse through the front page in order to truly take in what was happening. He was shocked. He felt as though he were about to faint due to feeling overwhelmed. He put the newspaper back down over the stack, unable to look at the picture of his smiling friend anymore, and turned to go home. His breathing became heavier, and upon returning home, he went upstairs to his bedroom, collapsed onto his bed, and wept loudly, dampening his pillow.

CHAPTER XIV

Monday was hard; Simon spent most of the day crying. He barely left his room, and only bothered to check the time in order to make it to the afternoon and evening services at synagogue early. He found it difficult to think straight, constantly worrying about Chaim.

The next morning, he thought about Chaim's family. Had any of them been taken captive too?

He phoned Mrs Spiegel and was relieved when she picked up. However, the relief wouldn't last very long, as Simon and Mrs Spiegel found themselves trying to work through a conversation while weeping.

'Everyone else is OK, thank God,' said Mrs Spiegel. She sniffed. 'He was in the south visiting his cousins in their kibbutz, where he was taken. We don't know what's happened to him. When the chag was over, I called him, but he didn't pick up.'

Simon listened to the dreadful news as tears continued to stream down his face. He wept in silence.

After speaking to Mrs Spiegel, he then spoke with Chaim's father, his older brother, Idan, and his younger sister, Tikva. It was very difficult and painful. They all cried as they spoke with him. Simon hung up in the end, after a phone call that had lasted for over half an hour.

It then dawned on Simon that the siyyum in which he had celebrated with Chaim just a couple of months ago might have been the last time he would have ever seen him. Then, he figured he should have hope; he didn't know what the future held. But the future seemed very bleak. Actually, the present looked very bleak.

He had a headache. He checked to see whether anyone had got back to him regarding his job applications, but not a single person had invited him for an interview. There were only some rejections.

Simon wondered as he sat down by his desk in his room: was this it? Would he never see Chaim again? Was he even alive? He didn't even know whether to begin the process of mourning. But that was it: he felt stuck. He wanted him to come back clear of any injuries, but what could he expect? When would he ever hear of him again? *Would* he ever hear of him again? Why would God put him through all this pain?

Later that evening, he heard the front door close downstairs. He sped down the stairs to see who it could be. He hadn't spoken to any of his housemates in days.

It was Asher and Naphtali. They sighed as they placed their instruments on the living room sofa.

'Hey, guys,' said Simon.

They barely looked at him.

'How are you?' asked Simon.

'Good,' replied Asher, but he didn't make eye contact.

'Where were you?' asked Simon.

Then he noticed that Naphtali had gone past him and into his room without saying a word to him.

'At Dan's house,' answered Asher.

Simon had noticed that Asher and Naphtali had been spending a lot of time out of the house lately.

'Were you guys hanging out?' he asked, wondering why he hadn't been asked along too.

'Nope,' said Asher, looking down as he continued to catch his breath, 'just rehearsing. We're a full, proper band now. We're getting ready to perform.'

Simon's jaw dropped.

'So, I take it that I,' he paused, 'won't be accepted into the band?'

'No, sorry, mate. I heard Yehuda had voted for you, just Dan and Adam said no. Adam said we already had an acoustic guitar player. Honestly, mate, I don't know why he'd ask you to audition if we've already got one.'

Asher was about to pass by Simon when Simon said, 'Yehuda voted for me?'

'Yeah, he did,' mumbled Asher.

Then, Asher finally went upstairs. This was it. Simon was not accepted into the band, the band he had come up with. He didn't know why Adam hadn't responded to any of his phone calls or text messages. He figured he would've felt bad breaking the news to him. By the look of it, maybe he had been too busy with all the rehearsals going on.

But finally, there was some good news. That night, Simon saw that one of the employers had responded to him, and he had been asked to attend an interview the following week.

CHAPTER XV

For the next few days, Simon couldn't help but notice that Asher and Naphtali seemed to be growing a little more distant. Sure, maybe they spent more time out rehearsing with the band, but even when they were in the house together, they didn't bother to have proper conversations with him. Reuben was the same way, except when he wasn't out, he tended to spend more time in his room.

Simon's life was becoming quieter. Rabbi Isaacs had left for Canada with his wife to spend some time with her family. Ezra had gone to Australia to visit relatives while on holiday. Simon would read the live updates on the BBC website and on the website of *The Times of Israel* to stay informed on the war with Hamas and to be aware of any news of the hostages. There was not a day that went by in which he didn't think about Chaim and the other hostages. Come to think of it, he realised that Chaim was actually his closest friend. He also came to realise that he hadn't told anyone about what had happened to Chaim, because no one had asked, and he hadn't been talking to so many people. Sometimes he would want to visit his parents, but he'd forget that they were working even though he wasn't. His father taught English and his mother art at the same Jewish day school in the neighbourhood. He still hadn't told them that he had lost his job.

On the morning of the job interview, Simon shaved and combed his hair. He was to meet the owner of the company at eleven o'clock. He had forgotten what it felt like to look forward to something – apart from Mashiach (the Messiah), Shabbat, and all the holidays – even though he was quite nervous. He dressed himself in his navy-blue suit, navy-blue trousers, and white shirt. He chose a purple tie, plain. He looked in the mirror and nodded; he was ready to go.

Simon took the tube to central London, where he met the employer in his office. He couldn't help but have a bad feeling throughout the interview. He answered all the questions to the best of his ability and honestly, yet he felt as though the boss – whose name he had quickly forgotten – was looking for something that simply wasn't there, and Simon felt as though he wasn't qualified due to his skillset and lack of experience. He shook hands with the owner after an interview that had lasted maybe around eight minutes and made his way across an office that carried an eerie silence as everyone dressed in more or less the same business casual uniform buzzed around efficiently carrying out their tasks.

He opened the glass door and took the lift back down to the ground floor, where he yet again found himself alone.

He didn't expect to get the job, if he were honest with himself. The owner hadn't appeared enthusiastic at all throughout the course of the interview, and Simon didn't think it was because he was trying to be serious in his consideration. He wouldn't have been surprised if there were a 'No Jokes Allowed' sign hanging somewhere in the office. He would've been surprised if he got the job, and he had the feeling he wouldn't enjoy working there if he did.

As the light flickered from '4' to '3' in the lift, he started to feel silly after having felt so optimistic about the new Jewish year. The year 5784 didn't owe him anything. God didn't owe him anything. He hadn't been entitled to being born. He was starting to feel that the whole 'be positive' mindset was a bit silly. It obviously didn't work; look where he was now. He was jobless, his best friend had been taken hostage by terrorists (though some weren't inclined to label them as such, which made him feel a lot better), and he was lonely. He was starting to wonder: had he any friends?

He thought about Reuben, how he would normally be considered by others to be too pessimistic, but maybe there was a certain wisdom to it. He had never seen Reuben surprised or disappointed; he had already expected worse things to happen, or at least, not much good. He wondered whether Reuben ever expected him to still be alive whenever he'd see him. Then he realised he was becoming negative in his thinking, engaging in thoughts of self-pity. He was shocked; he was becoming almost as negative as Reuben.

Upon exiting the office block, the delight of the cool, fresh autumn air and gentle breeze was interrupted as just down the street he encountered a sea of protesters on his way to the Underground station. There were Palestinian flags waving around, and though Simon would've normally felt intimidated by this presence, perhaps with everything going on in his life, he felt heartbroken; he thought of Chaim, and his eyes were starting to grow moist.

They started chanting things such as 'From the river to the sea'. Although Simon knew what it meant, for the first time he imagined it meaning from the River Thames to the North Sea, as well as the rest of Britain. He wondered how Brits would feel if another people wanted to take over their land. They'd just have to be OK with it.

As he made his way around the obstacle to his destination, a man started shouting at him, probably because he was the only person wearing a kippah in sight, which showed just how civil the protesters were.

Simon's heart started racing; he imagined the whole crowd rushing to turn on him, but he kept a stiff upper lip; maybe he had just gone numb after the past several weeks.

'You're stealing our land!' shouted the protester.

'Pardon?' said Simon, stopping, more because he didn't understand the man's argument than because he hadn't heard what he had just shouted within a few metres away. His parents would've suffered three panic attacks had they heard how he was engaging with the protester, but he was starting to think of this as fun; he had nothing else to do.

'You're stealing our land!' the protestor repeated. 'Thieves!'

Simon couldn't recall stealing any land; he wondered how he'd pay rent for his room in the house for another year. If he was referring to the Jews having the land of Israel, that was a fact attested to in the Bible, the same book where there was the narrative of Abraham's purchase of the Cave of Machpelah, but he knew the man wouldn't give in and go home after hearing this. He was being disingenuous for his own amusement. It was a relief after all the pain and suffering he had been going through.

Others around the protester noticed and started booing Simon with their thumbs pointed down.

'What land did I steal?' enquired Simon.

'The land of Palestine!' shouted the protester.

'I'm afraid you are mistaken,' explained Simon. 'I prefer Iraq.'

The man paused, looking clueless, as did the others around him, and that was when Simon took his leave and went home.

CHAPTER XVI

Simon had no desire to play his guitar or make new music. He missed Rabbi Isaacs' weekly class while he was away. He also missed the Tea and Torah programme he and Ezra had started. While passing by the kitchen window, he noticed that some weeds were starting to sprout in the garden. He wondered why he was always the one who had to tend the garden. Then, he remembered that he was the only one who had ever done it, and he had never asked anyone else to, nor had he ever hired a gardener.

He would leave the dishes on the dining table for hours after eating, and he would leave dirty dishes in the sink for days. He realised that he was doing exactly what he had rebuked Reuben for doing. He hoped that he wouldn't criticise him for that.

He got a text message from Matthew one day, asking whether he'd like to meet. Simon agreed and suggested that he should visit him at his place as he preferred not to go out. Matthew agreed and came over about two hours later. Simon was a bit embarrassed by the accumulating mess on the living room floor.

'How are you? How's the job search going?' asked Matthew, taking a cup of tea from Simon.

'I haven't applied to any job in weeks,' replied Simon.

'Why?' asked Matthew.

Simon shrugged.

'I hear you're part of the new band,' he said. 'Did you not get in after your audition?'

'Audition?' asked Matthew.

'Yeah.'

'What audition?'

'Didn't you audition to get into the band?'

'No.'

'I did.'

'Well, no one else did,' said Matthew.

Simon thought it was twisted that Adam would only have him audition – on top of that, to reject him on the basis of already having an acoustic guitar player when he had known he would audition for that position.

'I actually came to talk to you about that,' said Matthew.

And that was when Patrick came. He meowed and then brushed his head and back against Matthew's navy-blue trousers, his fur falling over his black shoes.

Matthew gasped in excitement.

'Oh, it's Pat the cat! Make sure you pet Pat!'

Matthew picked him up, and he immediately started purring as he placed him on his lap and petted his back.

'Have you got a cat?' asked Simon.

'No, I haven't, but I'd like to have one,' said Matthew. 'My family is more into dogs.'

'Ah,' uttered Simon, staring at Patrick, who blinked as he relaxed his face. He looked more content than Simon had been for ages.

'You wanted to talk about the band?' continued Simon.

'Yes,' said Matthew. 'We didn't have to audition, we just got in. He's the manager of the band, but we were all part of forming it because, well, we were just part of it. But I chose to leave. Adam sort of rubbed me the wrong way. I didn't get a good feeling about him. It's hard to explain, but then he started spreading rumours, and that's when I knew I had to leave.'

'Rumours?' said Simon.

'Yes,' said Matthew, nodding, then looking at Simon, 'about you.'

'Me?' exclaimed Simon, never having felt so important in his entire life.

'Yes, well, he's been saying all sorts of things for a while now. I now don't even hang out as much with everyone else because it's just become so toxic.'

'You guys hang out? I thought they've just been rehearsing.' Simon recalled having seen an advert at the kosher supermarket for their upcoming performance at a local venue.

'No, we hang out sometimes, too,' said Matthew.

Simon then had a stronger feeling that his housemates Asher and Naphtali had indeed been distancing themselves from him. He wondered if all his other friends in the band had been doing so intentionally as well.

'What has he been saying?' asked Simon.

'Just a whole bunch of things,' said Matthew. 'Things you've said, that Dan isn't a good singer, I can't play the guitar, Yehuda's bad at drums.' He noticed that Simon's jaw had dropped. 'I knew it was all rubbish.'

Simon couldn't remember exactly, but though he did admire Matthew's guitar skills and would never speak badly about that, he did recall having a conversation with Adam regarding his opinions on some of the band members' musicianship. His head started to hurt as his heart rate went up. He had to put the cup of tea down.

'Thank you for not believing that,' said Simon.

'Yeah, but I left early on,' Matthew pointed out. 'I'm not aware of whatever else he's said about you –'

'OK, thank you, Matthew,' said Simon, nodding, signifying that he had heard enough. He saw that Matthew had finished his cup of tea.

'Would you like more tea?' asked Simon.

'I would love some, if you don't mind,' replied Matthew.

'Not at all, my pleasure,' said Simon, getting up from the sofa to grab the empty teacup.

He went to the kitchen to turn on the electric kettle. Patrick hopped off Matthew's knees and followed Simon into the kitchen, brushing his head vibrating from purring against his black trousers.

Simon then realised he hadn't fed him all day. He felt horrible.

'I'm so sorry, Patrick,' he said, filling his empty purple tray with food.

Patrick then broke his fast.

Simon couldn't believe he had forgotten to feed poor Patrick. He grabbed the kettle filled with boiling water and poured it into the teacup, then placed the teabag in – which was illegal in Britain – after having forgotten to place it in there first.

That was when he heard the doorbell ring.

'I'll get it,' announced Matthew, which allowed Simon to disregard it.

He heard Matthew open the front door. He heard a man asking for tzedakah, or charity, as he had just lost his job and was struggling to pay for his boys' tuition for yeshiva.

'Er, sorry,' responded Matthew.

That was when Simon rushed to the front door, which Matthew had just closed.

Simon opened the door, passing a perplexed Matthew, and saw that the man was still on the pavement just in front of the house, making his way to his neighbour.

Simon ran up to him and grabbed a five-pound note from his pocket.

'Hi, sir. Sorry, my friend didn't quite understand. Here you go,' he said, handing him the note.

The bespectacled man, dressed in a black hat and black coat, thanked him and gave him a blessing for good health and success.

'Amen,' answered Simon. He grinned and made his way back to his house. Matthew had been standing in the doorway the whole time, watching everything.

'Who was that?' asked Matthew.

Simon closed the front door and they headed to the kitchen, where Patrick was feasting away.

'I don't know. He was asking for money,' said Simon.

'Oh, I got a bit nervous, and it's not my home, so I thought he was looking for someone. I feel bad,' said Matthew.

'No, that's fine, not to worry,' said Simon as he poured some milk into the tea and handed the teacup to Matthew.

'Cheers,' said Matthew.

'Pleasure.'

They returned to the living room. Matthew balanced the beverage in his hand as he skirted the two large sofa pillows lying on the floor to get to where he had been sitting by the bright window.

'Wow, so you just gave a random stranger money after he came to your place?' asked Matthew.

'Yeah,' Simon said casually. 'He probably saw the mezuzah on the door and assumed there were some Jews living here who would like to give. Charity is one of the commandments we have to follow.'

'Ah,' uttered Matthew, nodding. 'Do we have any commandments? Do gentiles have to do anything, or is it only for Jews?'

Simon knew that Matthew had been raised Anglican, but he wasn't really religious, unless it involved receiving presents on Christmas and eating on Easter.

'Well, there are the seven Noahide Laws which were given to all the gentiles, but the six hundred and thirteen commandments are for the Jews to follow,' said Simon, sipping his tea.

'And what are the seven Noahide Laws? What do they entail?' asked Matthew.

'Oh, murder, idolatry, adultery, stealing. Those are some of the things that are forbidden for gentiles to do,' Simon said casually.

'Fascinating. Haven't done any of that,' said Matthew, smiling and then getting to his feet just as a satisfied Patrick made his reappearance in the room. 'Thank you so much for having me.'

'Thanks for coming,' said Simon. 'I really appreciate it and I appreciate you telling me what's been going on.'

'Oh, you're welcome,' said Matthew.

Simon and Patrick saw him out.

After Matthew had left, Simon sat where Matthew had been sitting while Patrick ascended the stairs to nap on Simon's bed.

Simon reflected amidst the silence. Adam had been spreading lies about things he had never said to his friends. What else had he been saying? It was no wonder his friends wouldn't talk to him. Still, he couldn't help but notice that not one of them – apart from Matthew – had questioned this or confirmed with Simon first if he had actually said these things before believing them. He thought about calling Yehuda, but he was probably rehearsing with the band or working late hours at his day job. He was starting to feel upset.

Later, when Asher and Naphtali came home, Simon identified their voices from his upstairs bedroom and rushed downstairs to them. They were in the living room. Naphtali had just hung his jacket and scarf on the coat rack. They both engaged in that behaviour in which they wouldn't acknowledge him upon seeing him, withholding eye contact.

'Guys, I need to tell you something,' announced Simon. They still didn't look. 'I don't know what Adam has been telling you, but I really like you guys and think you're both very talented musicians.'

'Great, thanks,' muttered Naphtali as he brushed past him to retire to his bedroom.

Simon looked at Asher, who looked back at him. He looked somewhat intimidated, as if his bodyguard had just abandoned him. He stood frozen in the middle of the living room.

'Asher, are you angry at me?'

Asher sighed as he looked down.

'Listen, mate. I'm sorry, but I'm very tired. I think I'll head to bed now.'

Simon sulked. He didn't know what to do. He had no idea what was going on. Asher went to his bedroom upstairs.

Simon had no idea where Reuben was. He couldn't speak to any of his housemates.

He stood in the living room, gazing at the place where Matthew had sat on the sofa earlier that day. He figured he would have to deal with the source of all his troubles – Adam, who had been spreading all these lies. He was ruining all the relationships he had been cultivating with his friends for years. He would have to confront him.

CHAPTER XVII

Simon didn't want to wait to confront Adam and end the source of the conflict between him and his friends. On the very next day after speaking with Matthew, he rang Yehuda. He wanted to clarify with him whatever rumours he had heard and resolve any conflicts, but it went straight to voicemail. He looked at the time indicated on his mobile screen. It was ten o'clock. Then he remembered that he was working now and thus probably too busy to speak.

He wanted to call Adam, but he figured he would have the same result. He decided to call him at noon in case he'd have lunch at the time. He could then leave a voicemail and allow him to call back when he was available next should he not pick up. So, he called him, and did exactly that.

Two hours passed by, and Adam hadn't responded. He probably hadn't felt the need to respond during his break, whenever that was, unless he had been too busy. Simon would wait until after business hours.

He spent the next several hours on the Internet, reading through live coverage on the war against Hamas and listening to BBC World Service on his laptop in case there were any updates on the hostages.

By six o'clock, Simon assumed he wasn't going to get a response from Adam any time soon. He felt as though he were ignoring him. A part of him felt silly for having waited for so long.

He rang Matthew.

'Hey, do you know anything about what Adam would be doing today? Is the band going to rehearse or something? I'd like to speak to him.'

'I've heard they're going to be rehearsing tonight,' said Matthew.

'Where?'

'I don't know. I can call and find out.'

'Please do,' Simon requested.

'I'll get back to you,' said Matthew.

Simon appreciated Matthew's efforts, though he did feel bizarre about tracking Adam down to confront him in person. He was not one to engage in interpersonal conflict and criticise people.

Less than half an hour later, Matthew called him back.

'They're rehearsing at Yehuda's house at seven thirty tonight,' said Matthew. 'But you should know, they've got their first performance tomorrow night. They've got a gig at a small restaurant, so they might be particularly busy.'

'Thank you,' said Simon.

His heart started racing. He knew he had to confront Adam, and he didn't want to delay this any further. He was too nervous to make supper, and he didn't have much of an appetite. He knew it wouldn't be ideal to approach Adam and articulate his concerns on an empty stomach, but it was a quarter past seven and there was not much he felt he could do.

Simon set off for Yehuda's house, a place he hadn't been to for weeks.

Mrs Levy opened the door and welcomed him into the house with a smile. Simon knew it might have been the only smile he'd receive tonight.

'Oh, welcome,' said Mrs Levy. 'I didn't expect to see you tonight. All the other guys are rehearsing in the living room.'

'Thank you,' said Simon, who awkwardly made his way there as if he had never been there before. Mrs Levy ascended the stairs and disappeared.

Everyone in the band had been playing some form of Jewish rock music in unison, until seconds after they caught sight of Simon, when they suddenly stopped, and the music vanished and every instrument's sound descended into silence.

Simon hadn't seen this many friends in the same room for ages.

Adam straightened up, looking as though he were a guard during his watch at a fortress – and Simon was the intruder (though as far as Simon knew, it was Yehuda's house, though upon further reflection, he had invited himself over, which was something he never did).

Seeing that no one was speaking as they stared at him, Simon decided he would be the one to break the silence. He looked at Adam.

'May I have a word with you?'

Perhaps because of the pressure of being surrounded by everyone present and the need to look courageous, Adam acquiesced and headed with Simon to the entrance, stopping there, though Simon would have preferred outside. It was probably because he had to get back to rehearsals. No one else in the living room spoke a word for a good minute. Simon hoped that they couldn't hear their conversation.

'I want you to know that I'm aware of what you've been doing, spreading rumours about me saying that the people in the band aren't good players,' said Simon.

Adam's dark eyes glared at him amidst the shadowy space. 'What do you mean?'

Simon started to feel intensely uncomfortable. The way Adam looked at him made him feel as if he were very hostile, though he couldn't remember having done anything wrong to him, apart from maybe taking away a few minutes of his rehearsal time.

'I've heard you've been telling others that I think that they're bad musicians, and I don't appreciate you telling lies. I –'

'But those aren't lies,' said Adam, staring down at Simon with his large eyes.

Simon was stumped. He felt as if he had been caught in his snare.

'Don't you recall having told me you think Dan's not the best at singing, and Yehuda not the best at drums, that Asher could use some more practice? These were your words, not mine.'

Adam gave Simon some time to think about it, and Simon did vaguely recall sharing with Adam some critique he had on some members of the band. He couldn't believe it. It was true, then. Adam must have sensed this through his eyes, because he said, 'I'm not making these things up,' before returning to the rest of the band and prompting them to continue playing.

Simon thought about it. It was true. Maybe he shouldn't have confronted Adam, then. It was no wonder he'd felt so uncomfortable about it. He shouldn't have come here.

He left the house and walked home. He kept thinking about the awkward moment that he had just had. He then remembered the reason why he had been so upset. He didn't appreciate Adam spreading those rumours, even if they were true. It was damaging his friendships with so many people. Maybe one reason he had gone to Yehuda's to confront Adam was because a part of him secretly still wanted to join the band.

Then he remembered that Matthew had claimed that Adam had told him he thought poorly of his guitar skills. This was a blatant lie. He admired him as a guitar player. Had he really spoken poorly of Asher and Yehuda? It had been so long since he'd had that conversation with Adam. If only he could remember.

At home, Simon kept ruminating over Adam and the short, though detailed, conversation he'd had with him. If only he'd remembered that lie Matthew had shared with him, he thought. If only he'd remembered or been quick enough to mention how offended he was that Adam had shared all those words with his friends, whether or not they were true. He almost wanted to go back and yell at him. He wanted to tell him that it had been his idea for them to form a band in the first place. It had just been that Adam had been the one to act upon it.

He then remembered his friends, amidst his growing fury. Why hadn't he clarified over there what he had really thought about them? That he really cared? It was only nine o'clock now. There was a chance they were still rehearsing. But they had all been there! He felt silly. He couldn't believe all this was actually happening. But then, he thought: why hadn't they approached him? Why hadn't any of them contacted him, or greeted him while he was there in the house? What was wrong with his life?

CHAPTER XVIII

Simon remembered that Yehuda had been the only person who had voted for him to be part of the band. Feeling desperate, he called Yehuda that Thursday, and as he didn't pick up, he decided to head to his house. He figured he was the person most likely to be receptive to him clarifying the truth behind any rumours.

At around six o'clock, he arrived at Yehuda's house, thinking he would've returned home from work by now. He rang the doorbell. No one came at first, so he knocked on the door, thinking perhaps the doorbell wasn't working.

Mrs Levy opened the door.

'Oh, hi,' she said, looking a bit startled by his sudden appearance.

'Hi,' said Simon, 'is Yehuda by any chance here?'

'I'll go and check,' she said, smiling politely and nodding as she left the door ajar and disappeared.

Simon thought it was rather odd that she had to go and check to see whether her own son was home. Wouldn't she know? But then he thought that maybe everyone in the family more or less kept to themselves while in the house, staying in their own rooms most of the time.

'He's not here, sorry,' she said just as she returned, smiling politely and with a sympathetic look on her face.

'Oh, that's all right,' said Simon, turning around to head back home.

'Sorry,' said Mrs Levy again. 'Goodnight.'

'Goodnight,' replied Simon.

As he walked home, he had an odd feeling that Yehuda was indeed home but didn't want to talk to him. What on earth had Adam told him? If this was indeed the case, then it would carry its own serious implications. But how could he know? He could only think of his sole ally who still – even if loosely – associated himself with the group, and that was Matthew.

So, he rang him, and he picked up.

'Could you do me a huge favour?' Simon said under his breath even though there was no one near him on the street and no one in sight who was connected to anyone involved in the situation. 'I need you to find out whether Yehuda is home right now, but please don't tell him I asked.'

'Sure,' said Matthew in an understanding tone. He didn't even ask any questions.

'Cheers,' said Simon, touched by his alacrity.

'No problem,' said Matthew.

Matthew must have known that things had become awkward between Simon and his friends, which was why he was so quick to agree to fulfil such an odd favour.

Simon didn't normally test his friends like this, but he was very curious to know Yehuda's sincerity in regard to their friendship.

Within minutes, even before Simon arrived home, Matthew called Simon back.

'Yes, he's home,' said Matthew.

Simon was heartbroken. He was even surprised by how magnified the sudden pain and shock that filled his chest were.

'Sorry, mate,' Simon heard Matthew say in his right ear. It was almost like he could read his mind and discern how he was feeling, even though he hadn't mentioned the reason for his request.

Simon appreciated the sympathy, but he was still speechless. Yehuda had deliberately avoided him. But maybe there had been a legitimate reason for this.

'What was he doing?' asked Simon after swallowing. Maybe he was seriously engaged in something.

'Not much, it seemed,' said Matthew. 'I didn't really ask him, though he did ask me why I asked him whether he was home, and then I had to come up with an excuse, so I said because I wanted to hang out, but I had to pretend like I had something else on, so I quickly said I couldn't after he said yes. He must think I've become very scatterbrained.'

Simon was hurt by the idea that not only was Yehuda avoiding him, but he was doing so at a time when he was willing to spend time with another friend.

'Thanks for your help,' said Simon, trying to hide the pain in his voice.

'Anytime, mate.'

So it was certain that Yehuda had been home and didn't want to see him. Asher and Naphtali were obviously not interested in speaking to him, and if the only judge who had voted for him to join the band refused to see him, how would

Dan have wanted to see him, who had allegedly voted for him not to join the band?

Simon felt awful. Things seemed to be getting only worse. And to make it even worse than that, it seemed as though every effort he made to make things better had only proved to be in vain. Why even try? he thought.

CHAPTER XIX

Simon now understood that Asher and Naphtali were purposefully avoiding him, so he did the same. The days rolled on by, one not particularly distinguishable from the next. He spent a Shabbat alone. He didn't know where any of his housemates were. He called Reuben, but he didn't pick up. He wondered if Adam had said anything bad about him.

He stopped checking for updates on the situation with the hostages. He just didn't know what to think of it anymore. He lost all hope. It didn't help to see Chaim's face on one of the 'Kidnapped' posters on the front of one of the shops. He spent less and less time learning Torah, seeing that Ezra was too busy to learn, and he spent most of the day feeling low and isolated.

One Thursday morning, he woke up and wondered what time it could be as the light of day filled his bedroom. He stayed in bed, wishing he could go back to sleep, which in a way transported him through time, allowing him to skip any possible misery and pain he would've felt. He had been quite lethargic lately. He got out of bed, figuring he wasn't tired enough for sleep, and discovered that it was nearly a quarter past noon. He had missed the morning service at synagogue again. He would have to don phylacteries.

He sat on the seat by his desk, staring absent-mindedly through the windows. Matthew called, but he didn't pick up. He had received a text message from him indicating that he'd like to meet, but Simon didn't want to. Matthew was a positive, happy young man, and he didn't want to ruin his disposition with his negativity. Ezra was still away. Rabbi Isaacs was still away. He hadn't had a proper conversation with anyone in days. Maybe he'd get a greeting from someone at synagogue or at the supermarket. Apart from that, he'd have no human interaction.

His books were gathering dust. He hadn't learnt Torah for over a week. His guitar was in its case hibernating.

He brushed his teeth and then returned to his bed, where he lay down, facing the windows.

Patrick came in and hopped onto the bed. He purred and brushed his face and whiskers against Simon's face and short sideburns and beard (he hadn't shaved for over a week).

Simon turned, facing the wall.

Patrick meowed and hopped over him, brushing his side against Simon's chest.

Simon had never recalled turning away from Patrick. He'd always welcome him and show affection, but this time, Patrick was starting to annoy him. He took him and placed him onto the floor next to the bed, then turned as he lay and buried his face into the blanket, darkening any brightness that his closed eyelids perceived.

Patrick meowed.

Simon turned over and looked at him. Patrick blinked. They would stare at each other for a good ten seconds, until Patrick decided it was time to lick his right paw.

Then, Simon felt terrible. He realised that he had forgotten to feed him that morning – again. He had to act this time and not just think things. He went downstairs into the kitchen and filled his tray with food.

Patrick ate.

Simon looked at all the dirty dishes that had sat in the kitchen for days.

He made himself a cup of tea and sighed. He stood by the back door as the steam of the tea swirled over the teacup. He looked outside, and saw that the garden had become infested with weeds. The uninvited green contrasted with the grey clouds above. Speaking of plants, his indoor plants were dying. He kept forgetting to water them. He didn't know if they'd survive.

Patrick brushed his cheek against his pyjamas.

'Do you realise how lucky you are?' asked Simon.

Patrick purred.

'You live like a king. I feed you, take care of you, give you shelter.'

Simon couldn't help but notice that Patrick had been living a content life. He received everything he ever wanted. Meanwhile, Simon, who was a human being, thus more distinguished and for whose kind the world had been created, was suffering, miserable, and stressed. Could he learn a thing or two from Patrick about how to be happy? He wasn't planning on having Reuben feed him cat food any time soon.

He couldn't look at the weeds anymore because it stressed him. Instead, he gazed up at the clouds as he took a sip of his tea. Patrick lay on his side beside his feet. Chaim was still missing. There had been no good news regarding the hostages. None of the jobs he had applied to had brought a response. There was absolutely nothing he could look forward to.

He looked down at Patrick, whose eyes were nearly shut.

His heart was starting to feel too heavy to carry around in his chest, and his brain was starting to feel cloudy as his thoughts weren't so clear and his capacity for intellectually engaging activities diminished. He stared through the window, and the steam that swirled over his tea appeared as though it combined with the fog that now descended upon the garden.

Simon looked down at Patrick again. He was now sleeping.

Simon's lip quivered as his throat contracted.

'I'm sorry to do this, Patrick,' he said, and Patrick awoke as he carried him upstairs and put him into his cage. He phoned his parents, asking if he could go to their house, and they said yes.

So, he got dressed and carried Patrick, who was meowing in his cage, and headed over to his parents' house. He went down less busy streets so as to avoid seeing any of his friends and unwanted attention from pedestrians due to Patrick's meows of protest.

Mr and Mrs Jacobs welcomed him in, then saw he'd brought Patrick.

'Oh, wanted to bring him for a visit?' asked Mr Jacobs.

Simon sniffed. He had fought hard not to sob on his way over here. His parents must have heard the emotion in his voice, because their facial expressions turned into ones of deep sympathy shortly after he had begun to speak.

'I can't keep doing this anymore,' explained Simon. 'I can't keep taking care of him. I keep forgetting to feed him in the mornings. I can't be there for him. He needs attention and I just can't do this anymore. I don't want him to feel bad. It's really hard, but it's what's best for him. Can you please take care of him?'

Patrick meowed as Simon felt him move around in his cage.

'Of course,' said Mr Jacobs.

'Are you all right?' asked Mrs Jacobs.

'Thank you,' said Simon, who laid down the cage. He opened it, and Patrick crept out, sniffing the carpeted floor, before speeding off down the corridor.

'I'm not feeling well,' Simon finally answered Mrs Jacobs.

'Why?' she asked.

'You know about Chaim,' he said. They nodded.

'Why don't you stay here for Shabbos?' suggested Mrs Jacobs.

They both looked at him with concerned faces.

Simon didn't know where everyone else in his house would be this Shabbat, but it wasn't like they would talk to him much if they were home, anyway. He figured he might as well be with people who cared about him.

He nodded.

CHAPTER XX

Simon did the shopping for his parents on Erev Shabbat, on Friday morning. He helped Mrs Jacobs cook cholent that afternoon. Plenty of steam rose from the pot of boiling water filled with beef brisket, beans, barley, potatoes, garlic and onions mixed with salt and pepper. Simon removed the layer of scum with a wooden spoon as Mrs Jacobs took out the fresh challah from the oven.

'Where's Reuben? Have you seen him?' asked Simon.

'He was last here a few days ago,' she answered.

That night, Simon and his parents sat by the dining table to eat. Simon was clean-shaven. It had been a bit more painful than usual to shave as his facial hair had grown a bit longer than he'd normally let it.

'Have you heard of Yehuda's band performing?' asked Mrs Jacobs. 'They've been doing shows around. I hear they're very good. What's their name again?'

'The Beis,' answered Mr Jacobs.

'Oh, that's right,' she said. 'Simon, why don't you try to join the band? Do you think you could ask them?'

'Mum, I don't want to talk about that right now,' he said. He looked down as he ate his chicken soup. Although his mother's chicken soup was delightful, he couldn't help but lower his head after carrying the stress he had felt throughout the whole week. He looked like one of his dehydrated, dying houseplants.

Mr and Mrs Jacobs kept eating their soup, seeing that Simon was clearly vexed.

'I heard you've lost your job,' said Mrs Jacobs.

Simon was shocked. He couldn't believe he hadn't told his parents after all these weeks. He hadn't meant to keep it a secret from them anymore; he had just forgotten to after everything else going on in his life.

'Yes,' he confirmed.

'So, what now?' she asked.

Simon shrugged, still staring at the yellow-coloured soup. 'I've applied for jobs, I had an interview, but I haven't had any offers yet.'

'Oh,' she said, sounding disappointed.

'Wait, who told you? Reuben?'

She nodded.

'Oh,' uttered Simon.

'He's been very down lately,' she said. 'I think you've hurt him.'

'What?' said Simon, genuinely shocked and confused.

'Yes,' she said. 'I think you've been very cruel to him. You don't let him hang out with you anymore. Why is that?'

'That's not my fault. I – my friends – I'd love to hang out with him. It's complicated.'

'OK, well, I think you should talk with him,' she suggested.

'He won't talk to me,' said Simon.

Mr and Mrs Jacobs exchanged brief glances of concern. They then finished their soup in silence, before changing the subject with the main course.

Later that night, Simon sat on the living room sofa as his father sat on another. Simon mostly skimmed through the latest issue of *The Jewish Chronicle* as his father learnt Rashi's commentary on the weekly parsha. Simon also reflected a lot on all the things going on in his life.

Mr Jacobs fixed his glasses, saying, 'Fascinating,' before getting up to place the book on the bookshelf.

'I hope you're not upset that I haven't told you until now that I've lost my job,' said Simon, as Mr Jacobs browsed through his bookshelf. 'I just didn't want you to be anxious.'

'Oh, Simon. You know your mother and I will always be anxious,' he said, smirking.

Simon could only feel pity after this comment.

'Ah,' uttered Mr Jacobs as he found a copy of the Gemara tractate on Shabbat and returned to his seat. 'I'm an anxious person, and your mother is an anxious person, and we were anxious to marry each other, so we were a perfect match.'

Simon now felt pity for both of them.

Later, he retired to the guest bedroom, where he would be sleeping that night. He had brought all of his essentials over. He had figured he wouldn't have to walk to his house after dinner and it would be nice to have a little escape. Not only that, but it would be nice to not have any possible awkward moments with his housemates. It surely felt as though everyone in the world was against him. He thought, was he a bad person? Only his parents seemed to like him, and they were supposed to.

He heard Patrick sneeze in the darkness of the room, the only light dimly filtering through the curtains from outside and creeping underneath the door to the corridor that came from the kitchen and living room. Patrick had spent most of the time hiding underneath the bed, only coming out to eat food which had to be placed out in the corridor close to the room. Apparently, after almost a whole year living with Simon at his house, he needed time to readjust to their old home.

Just when bad news seemed to stop streaming constantly into Simon's life, when it felt like he could breathe for just a moment, he was reading in the living room the next morning as he and Mrs Jacobs were waiting for Mr Jacobs to come home from synagogue when Mrs Jacobs came into the living room and said, 'You know, I haven't told you, but Mum has Covid.'

'What?' uttered Simon, sounding more annoyed than concerned.

'Yes,' she confirmed, nodding. 'She's not doing very well. I found out yesterday. I didn't want to tell you because you seemed a bit down.'

Mrs Jacobs spoke these words while appearing rather worried, but Simon started crying. He just felt helpless. He wept and couldn't even move to get up and grab some tissues.

Mrs Jacobs looked heartbroken as Simon sat there crying. He couldn't even think about his grandmother being ill. Not now.

Then Mr Jacobs arrived home. He didn't notice Simon crying as he met his wife in the kitchen. He then noticed, but pretended not to, wanting to give Simon some privacy.

No one mentioned Simon crying or what the cause could've been throughout the rest of Shabbat. Even during lunch, Simon wondered what his mother would ask next regarding his sudden emotional outburst, or whether his father had noticed, but they just spoke about other things. He couldn't even remember the last time he had cried in front of them. He must've been around five years old.

Simon now felt anxious to be in his own parents' house. It was like doom was his only fortune. It felt as though his life was consuming itself, imploding. After Shabbat ended, he returned to the guest room and gathered his belongings, though Patrick, still hiding under the bed, would not be coming with him. What would he do? he thought. He had no idea what to expect. His future appeared blank, just black, as if nothing could happen. He couldn't expect anything now. He had no plans for the next week. He didn't know what to do.

He started as his mother knocked on the door.

'May I have a word with you?' she asked.

'Sure,' said Simon, laying the navy-blue suit he'd wear on Shabbat down on the bed. He felt a heavy pressure in his chest. He grew tense, bracing himself for more bad news.

Mrs Jacobs sat down on the bed, and Simon did the same next to her.

'Are you all right?' she asked.

Simon looked down at the beige-coloured carpet. There was only one right answer.

'No.'

'What's wrong?'

Simon sighed. He had a headache again and thought about how to answer. Where was he to begin?

'Everything.'

Mrs Jacobs thought for a moment.

'Maybe you need to get away for a little bit, something different to get your mind off things.'

Simon thought about it. Yes, that makes sense, he thought. All of his troubles, all of the people he was in conflict with, existed in this area. If he could just get away, he'd be able to put it all out of his mind. But where would he go? He hadn't thought of travelling. He thought about going to Israel, but there was the war, and not only was he too afraid to go, but his parents would probably lose their minds, God forbid, and he had already lost his, so he needed to rely on them to stay sane, as unlikely as that was.

'Where should I go?' he asked.

'I have a cousin who lives in America,' she said. 'Do you remember Rivka?'

Simon hadn't seen Rivka since he was six years old, and that was when his maternal uncle had got married in Manchester.

'Yes.'

'You could stay with her for a bit. I'll call her. Let's see. It's still Shabbos there right now. If I'm still up later, I'll call her. If not, I'll call her tomorrow and let you know.'

'Where in America does she live?'

'In New York.'

Simon thought about it, then nodded.

'OK.'

As he walked back home that night, he started to cry. Patrick wouldn't be living with him for the time being. He was too distraught to take care of him. It would be too painful to forget feeding him again. He already missed him. The darkness of night masked his tears from the public, and he avoided the main road again, lest he see one of his friends. He wasn't ready to encounter them, and, thankfully, he didn't.

CHAPTER XXI

After about an eight-hour flight, which didn't include delays before takeoff, Simon finally arrived at John F. Kennedy International Airport at a little past noon. He was feeling very fatigued. He hadn't slept a minute during the flight; he had an aisle seat and the man taking the middle seat next to him kept rebuking his kids who sat in the row ahead for causing too much noise and not keeping still, while his daughter, who had the window seat next to him, complained the whole time about virtually everything. He had only ever travelled internationally to Israel. While he'd hear American accents occasionally in central London and on rare occasions even in Golders Green, he had never experienced such a high concentration of them before being in this aeroplane, but that wouldn't have prepared him for when he arrived; he had suddenly become the only Brit in the vicinity and was starting to feel self-conscious about his own British accent. At least in Israel, he spoke Hebrew more or less fluently.

He took a taxi to his relatives' residence in the neighbourhood of Fresh Meadows, in the borough of Queens. This was apparently in another part of New York City, which was quite big.

He gazed at all the tall buildings as he rode there; they were quite wide, too. He was starting to feel rather small, and that his many problems were quite small, too, compared to the rest of the universe. Then he saw on the news on his mobile that there was a pro-Palestinian protest taking place in Times Square. He sighed. He had come all the way here to run away from his problems, and before he could even make it to his destination, there were his problems, too. He figured his problems would follow him everywhere.

After taking so long to leave the aeroplane, exit the airport, find a taxi, and arrive at Fresh Meadows, the cloudy sky was starting to darken. He saw that he had brought the weather from Britain with him too. He wouldn't be surprised if the Americans would start protesting against him as well. He had seen a synagogue on the ride to the house, and it wasn't so far, so he walked back to where he had spotted it, which took about ten minutes. He entered and left his suitcase in the coat room so he could attend the afternoon service. He let his mother's cousin know that he had arrived and was at synagogue. The rabbi gave a class on the weekly Torah portion with Ramban's commentary, and then there was the evening service.

Simon struggled to keep his eyes open. Outside it was dark, but somehow, he was able to schlep the suitcase back to where his relatives' house was even though it was his first time there.

He knocked on the door, nervous to meet his relatives. His mother's cousin-in-law, Mr Lieberman, opened the door.

'Ah, Simon, so good to see you!'

They embraced. It was the first time Simon had met Mr Lieberman.

Mr Lieberman escorted him to the corridor. Simon tried to answer his questions to the best of his ability – how the flight was, what he thought about America (he had been here for less than eight hours, and he still couldn't believe he was here), how each and every member of his family was doing – all while rolling his suitcase up to the entrance of the guest room where he'd be staying. He had never interacted with someone with such a thick New York accent before.

He participated (unwillingly) in the interview with the closed wooden door of the guest room, which indicated paradise to him as all he wanted to do was lie down and slumber, right next to him. Then Mrs Lieberman came out into the corridor from her room and greeted Simon with much enthusiasm.

'Simon! How are you?' she asked, before proceeding to ask him virtually the same questions that Mr Lieberman had. Right, it makes sense that they're married, thought Simon.

'The kids are so excited to meet you!' said Mrs Lieberman. 'They've been talking about it all week!'

Simon tried to smile, worried that he would have to meet them as well before finally being able to get some sleep.

'Right, well, I look forward to meeting them as well.'

'Good,' she said, grinning, 'I love the British accent.'

Simon blushed, though he thought it was rather funny.

'Well, there isn't one British accent,' he pointed out. 'There's Cockney, Geordie, Estuary, and RP, which you may associate with films or the BBC,' he said, but he paused, as Mrs Lieberman appeared to grin oddly with an expression that seemed to indicate a mixture of politeness and shock. It was as if she had never been corrected in her entire life for being wrong, as if she *couldn't* be wrong.

'Well, I think she meant British accents in general,' said Mr Lieberman, to save her, Simon assumed.

'We're going to have dinner soon, so you'll be able to meet the kids then,' she announced, almost as though Simon had come to a weekend retreat rather than visiting relatives.

'Oh, lovely. I look forward to it,' said Simon.

Mr and Mrs Lieberman finally left him and he collapsed onto the bed, forgetting to close the bedroom door and turn off the lamp he had turned on.

He slept until eleven o'clock the next morning, then fell under another spell of sleep, waking up after noon.

Someone had been kind enough to turn off the lamp, but left the door open for some reason. Simon guessed it had been to help him wake up as it was so late, but then that person would've kept the lamp on.

Although the corridor had been beaming with light the first time he had woken up, there was something different the second time: pots and pans were clattering in the kitchen and water was running in the sink.

He sighed. He had missed the morning service again, even in America. He had also wanted to visit Times Square, but he wasn't sure if he'd have enough time before Shabbat. He wondered whether there was another protest at Times Square; one cheeky exchange with a protester had been enough for a lifetime.

Seeing that he didn't have to change into proper clothing from his pyjamas as he had slept in the clothes he had travelled in, he simply got up and emerged from the guest room.

In the kitchen, Mrs Lieberman was washing meat. The smell of chicken soup and challah filled the air.

'Good morning,' said Simon.

Mrs Lieberman jumped.

'Oh! You scared me. I see you've missed shacharis,' she said, denoting the morning service at synagogue.

Simon felt terrible.

'Yes,' he mumbled.

'Well, please make yourself at home. Would you like something to drink? Are you hungry?'

'Sure, I'll take some tea, please.'

'Sure.'

'Have you got porridge?'

'I'm sorry? – I don't think so,' answered his aunt while trying to attend to the pot of soup.

'OK,' he said, then waited, wondering if she had understood him. He wondered if maybe in America, the guest had to find the tea himself, then use the kettle on his own. Maybe there was a distinct place in the kitchen where they kept their tea. But then, as if she had just remembered, his aunt took out a mug and teabag from a cupboard, and prepared the tea with an electric kettle, which took several minutes as she had other ongoing duties. Simon would've offered to do it himself, but he felt intimidated by her robust industriousness in the kitchen. He didn't want to interfere with her in her own workshop.

Simon drank his tea, which was actually green rather than black, and with a lot more sugar than he could've asked for, and he never took his tea with sugar. He struggled to finish it, hiding his winces from his aunt as he sat by the white round table in the kitchen. The excess sugar couldn't mask the bitterness of the tea. At least, by the smell of it, there was good food to look forward to. He was still waiting to meet his younger cousins. He had no idea how many children Mrs Lieberman had.

He roamed around the ground floor of the house, admiring the collection of books in the living room. The house was so big compared to the average home in England. Even the rooms were big. He noticed that there was a staircase that led to a second floor as well as one that led to a rather large looking basement. He imagined hidden bedrooms being there, too.

Upon returning to the guest room, he noticed he had received a voicemail from his anxious mother. As she was five hours ahead, it was already Shabbat in Britain, so he couldn't call her back to let her know he was still alive. Or at least he could, but she wouldn't pick up. He listened to the voicemail:

'Simon, how are you? I've tried calling you so many times. Have you arrived at the airport? Are you OK? Please call me. By the way, I'm not sure if you want to hear this, but I'll tell you. Yehuda's band – what's it called, The Beis? – they're actually going to New York! I'm not sure if they're there now, but they'll be performing at a few places for a while. I'm not sure how long. By the way, did you know that Chaim's brother is in the IDF and fighting in Gaza? All right, well, please call me back.'

That message had been received last night at around nine o'clock. Simon's consciousness had already drifted to another world by then. She must've been worried sick by now, and there was no way to notify her of his well-being at this point. He felt very bad and worried about her; she'd have to go through Shabbat wondering whether he was alive. Though he figured that this was what Chaim's parents felt about their son every day now.

He started thinking about Chaim, and his heart felt broken again. Travelling to another country had changed nothing. And the band was here! What were they doing here, and why did they have to be in New York City while he was here? Sure, it was an international city, but there were hundreds, if not thousands of other cities in the world!

He felt awful knowing the band was currently in the same city as him. Indeed, his problems had followed him from Britain. He started feeling a headache coming on again. He was also hungry, and felt weak and fatigued, though he was looking forward to the meal he'd have tonight for Shabbat.

He showered and got dressed and figured the family would notify him soon when they'd be heading off to synagogue.

One of his cousins (he presumed) came by. He looked to be a teenager. He wore an untucked white shirt and tzitzit, or fringes, hanging out, the white tzitzit contrasting with his black trousers. He was slim and of average height, though shorter than Simon by a bit.

'Hi, are you Simon?' he asked excitedly.

'Yes.'

'I'm Menashe. Is this your first time in the US?'

'Yes.'

'Wow, cool. We're going soon to shul. Want to play chess?'

'Sure.'

The two of them headed to the round table in the kitchen where Menashe started setting up the board.

'I'll be black,' said Simon, seeing that most of the scattered black pieces were closer to him.

He heard Menashe utter a strange noise, sounding almost like a gulp, and looked up to find him wide-eyed, his jaw dropped. Simon wondered if he had said or done something.

The game was set up, so he added, 'So, you go first. You're white. Or is it different in America?'

Simon genuinely wondered whether black went first in America. Menashe looked as though he were about to have a panic attack, which truly made him his cousin, with every word that came out of his mouth.

'Are you OK?' asked Simon.

'Yeah,' said Menashe, before finally moving one of his middle pawns two squares forward.

Simon lost just in time before Mr Lieberman announced that he was ready to go to synagogue. Two younger cousins of Simon appeared already in their suits and waiting to leave.

They went to synagogue, and returned home for dinner. Mr Lieberman's mother, who lived nearby, was there for dinner. When she spoke, something about her dismal voice and demeanour seemed to display a plea for compassion, as if life had been too difficult, and that one ought not to be too hard on her. Simon could relate to the feeling. Simon struggled to keep up with the two simultaneous conversations unfolding to his right and left as he sat at the centre of the table. It turned out that Menashe was seventeen years old and had three younger brothers and a younger sister. He felt somewhat invisible throughout the meal, not knowing the people or understanding the contexts of the various politics, community affairs, friends, relatives, or neighbours they were talking about.

After reciting grace after meals, Simon noticed he was starting to feel a little less tired, maybe after all the energy from the food. He looked at the digital clock on the oven. If it was correct, it was half past nine, which meant that his body was probably functioning as though it were half past two in the morning. He didn't want to think about this concept for too long.

Menashe came in with his eleven-year-old brother, Yehoshua, putting on his black overcoat.

'Want to come to shul with me?' asked Menashe. 'Me and my friends study there every Shabbos night. You should come!'

Seeing that Simon wasn't desperate for sleep for the first time during his sojourn in America, he accepted the invitation. He wondered if he'd make it to the morning service at synagogue the next day.

He, Menashe, and Yehoshua made their way in that chilly, windy night in their coats across the neighbourhood to arrive at this particular synagogue, which was different from the one Simon had been praying in.

There was a small, bright study hall with a few dozen men, mostly teenagers, in groups, who learnt and conversed. There was plenty of cholent and potato kugel being served in plastic bowls, but at this point, Simon couldn't tolerate any more food. Apparently, all the boys here had unlimited tolerance.

Yehoshua immediately separated from them and sat with some boys looking to be around his age. Menashe and Simon sat at another table with five other guys around Menashe's age.

'This is The Happy Club!' said Menashe, grinning. 'Welcome. Guys, this is my cousin, Simon. Would you like to join?'

'Er, I beg your pardon?' asked Simon, who had simply wanted to tag along, not sell his soul to any organisation.

'We're The Happy Club! We're all things positivity, and we meet here and learn Torah and be happy.'

'That sounds like a ridiculous concept,' said Simon, then paused. Had he actually said that? He was somewhat amazed at how easily the words had rolled off his tongue. Maybe it was the jet lag? He would have never given such a harsh, blunt critique about anything usually. Although it was his honest opinion about the group, he hadn't meant to say it. He saw the surprised and nervous looks on their silent faces. He was just about to apologise when Menashe leant over.

'Can I talk with you for a second?' he asked under his breath so that his happy friends couldn't hear.

'Sure,' said Simon.

As he followed his seventeen-year-old cousin out of the study hall mostly filled with kids just over half his age, he couldn't help but think that there was something mentally wrong with him. He was certainly being handled as though he belonged in an asylum.

Menashe spoke with him gently in the corridor by the wall.

'I know you're new here, but we can't have you behave this way. Even if you want to be a guest, you can't be acting this way. You have to be positive in our meeting, or else you can't be part of it.'

'OK,' Simon heard himself say, wondering if he had died in a plane crash. If this was his share in the World to Come, he had seriously needed to work harder.

He followed his cousin back into the study hall and resolved not to speak another word so as to ensure he wasn't banished from the group, not knowing who else he could talk to here. That evening, he stayed there for two hours, listening to them learn Gemara and talk about food. He would've left earlier, but he had forgotten the way back home and needed shelter tonight; he wasn't taking risks with the only form of security he had left. The only way he was able to evade another private intervention or outright banishment was by not uttering another word.

After the incarceration, Simon, Menashe, and Menashe's happy friends put on their coats in the coat room and made their way towards the exit.

Simon stopped by the door.

'Isn't Yehoshua coming?' he asked Menashe.

'Oh, he usually goes with his friends. It's OK; they walk together and one of them lives down the block.'

'OK,' uttered Simon, following them. It had been a long way here. It had almost taken fifteen minutes to get here, but he took Menashe's word for it.

Eventually, Menashe's friends separated from the group when they approached the streets they lived on, and only Simon and Menashe were left as they walked down a street so wide it had numerous lanes.

Simon shivered as the night grew colder and the winds picked up.

They stopped at a corner. The pedestrian sign featured a red hand. Then, it featured a white man.

'Oh, you've got a white man here.'

As they crossed the zebra crossing, Menashe suddenly looked like he was having a seizure.

'Er, we have a green one in England,' he quickly added. 'And you've got a red hand to stop, whereas we've got a red man.' Thank God, Menashe seemed to be calming down.

Simon was only making an innocent observation, but Menashe seemed to get quite defensive.

'Well, it makes sense. The red hand is to stop, whereas the walking man means to walk,' he argued.

Simon nodded. He wasn't sure whether to respond, seeing that he had unintentionally got himself involved in a quarrel, but, nonetheless, he said, 'But it's simpler with two similar figures, isn't it? One is red for not walking, one green for walking, like the traffic lights. Red is for stopping, green for going. You don't have a red hand and a white car.'

'I guess,' Menashe said defeatedly, his head lowered. Simon was a bit confused. Menashe had been speaking as if the pedestrian signs here were clearly the right and only way to go about it; Simon had simply wanted to show him how another system worked. He had never intended to start a debate to prove how anyone's system was the ideal way.

The silence that took hold within the next few minutes must have been a sign of Menashe's new disapproval of Simon. He felt it. Simon's night had been full of perplexities, but that seemed to be the case for his life in general, anyway.

'What exactly is the purpose of The Happy Club?' he asked after a while, aware Menashe might ignore him forever (he was good at eliciting that response in people, apparently).

'We have to serve Hashem with joy,' said Menashe, still sounding a bit grumpy as he looked down at the pavement. 'We started it three years ago.'

Simon felt terrible. He had no idea that Menashe had been suffering for three years.

'So,' Menashe continued, 'we decided we would create a club dedicated to happiness. We would be positive. It's every Friday night we meet. It's like we're being spiritual coaches for each other, lifting ourselves up, supporting each other, encouraging each other. It's relieving that no matter how difficult your week is, we can come together and just be positive. So far, people have joined and loved it – you were the only one to reject being invited.'

Menashe's eyes sneered at Simon, but Simon pretended something ahead had suddenly caught his attention.

'You aren't allowed to complain or do or say anything negative,' explained Menashe. 'It actually gets a lot easier once you get used to it.'

'But don't you think it's a bit unrealistic?' asked Simon, fully aware of the impending ostracism. 'You're bound to have a bad day at some point or other.'

'Oh, you could have a bad day,' said Menashe, almost as if he were giving Simon permission for a reality he had already long possessed, 'but you just can't be negative during the meeting. It's only on Friday nights.'

Simon still had doubts about the club, and he enjoyed having these doubts.

Shortly after returning home, all was quiet and Simon was reading by the kitchen table after Menashe had left the kitchen. Yehoshua entered and greeted Simon with a smile.

'Gut Shabbos,' he said.

'Gut Shabbos,' responded Simon, closing the *Ami Magazine*.

Yehoshua took the seat next to him. He was catching his breath after walking in the cold night air.

'I see you were in The Happy Club,' remarked Yehoshua.

'Just as a sad, quiet guest,' replied Simon, browsing through the contents of the magazine again.

'I used to be in The Happy Club,' Yehoshua said, as if that were a good thing.

Simon looked at him as he stared down at the floor, swinging his feet by the chair. 'Were you?'

'Yeah, but I got kicked out.'

Simon couldn't believe it. Yehoshua seemed to smile more than Menashe ever did.

'Why?'

'I complained about yeshiva being hard. Then, they gave me a warning. Then, a few weeks later, I accidentally talked about my head hurting because I was sick the whole week, and then they kicked me out.'

Seeing how sad Yehoshua looked, Simon wanted to cry for his younger cousin, only because he had bought into such utter rubbish.

'That's just twisted,' he remarked, even as Menashe walked back into the kitchen. He suddenly had a deeper level of pity for his cousins.

'What does that mean?' asked Yehoshua.

'Wrong, messed up,' Simon elaborated.

'I like your accent,' remarked Yehoshua.

And that was the end of their conversation. When Simon later went to sleep, it felt as if he had already been dreaming for quite some time.

CHAPTER XXII

Simon was unaware of the context of half of the conversations during the two remaining Shabbat meals. Menashe seemed not to be annoyed with him anymore, as he was talking to him on Shabbat day. This didn't stop Simon from feeling bad for him and Yehoshua. Needless to say, there was no more mention of his club.

After Shabbat ended and Simon made havdallah with the Liebermans in their home, he thought it would be nice to explore the city, and thought to visit Brooklyn as there were so many Jews who lived there, though he was unaware of the neighbourhoods, so he asked Mrs Lieberman for suggestions.

'Well, there's Williamsburg, Borough Park, Crown Heights...'

'Isn't the Chabad Headquarters in Crown Heights?' asked Simon.

'Yes,' she said.

So, upon Simon's request, she handed Simon a map of the subway and he determined to visit the iconic 770. He dotted the exact location based on where Mrs Lieberman had pointed it out with a pen on the map, and he rode on the New York City subway system for the first time that night. He also had to take a bus along the way due to his location in Queens. For the first time in a while, he was feeling a little excited about something, but this quickly dissipated. What if he were to bump into the members of the band? New York City was huge. The odds were so low. But with his luck, maybe the band would be performing at 770.

The journey took almost two hours. It would've been a lot quicker by taxi (though more expensive), but he didn't mind. He wanted to experience public transport in New York City. He also enjoyed the views offered on the bus ride, as well as seeing what the New York City subway system looked like, though it was quite dirty. He emerged from the subway station and walked through the neighbourhood of Crown Heights.

He saw Hasidic Jews walking around. It took him longer than expected to find 770. Finally, he mustered up the courage to ask someone for help, who then pointed towards the right direction to walk down Eastern Parkway. This then turned into a conversation that lasted for twenty minutes, as the young man was curious as to where Simon was from, probably due to his accent and because he was wearing a peacoat and navy-blue chinos and kippah now that it was no longer Shabbat, rather than his Shabbat suit and trousers, contrasting him with the man's black hat, long, black coat, and long beard and payot, or sidelocks, and he spoke with a Yiddish accent, had dark hair, and wore glasses. Apart from Simon's British accent, he was clean-shaven, wore black derbies, and had long, straight, brown hair. He couldn't be more different from the man in physical appearance. He answered his questions on where he went to yeshiva, where in England he was from, and what he worked as (happily unemployed).

After the conversation was over, Simon headed down Eastern Parkway. It was nighttime, and he wasn't familiar with how the headquarters looked. He had walked in the direction the man had indicated, but he had the feeling he had walked too far. It had been almost twenty minutes since he had spoken with the man. It was getting very late now, and there weren't as many people walking outside. He could've passed 770 without even knowing. Instead, he went down another street and decided he'd just explore Crown Heights, and if he passed the perimeter, Brooklyn in general.

Several minutes passed, and everything was starting to grow quiet. Many of the shops had closed. The streetlights made everything visible. There were even fewer people out. In fact, Simon hadn't seen anyone for a while now. He was heading northwards. It was too quiet, like the city that never sleeps was now sleeping. Maybe there had been another wave of Covid and the whole city had been placed under curfew, and here he was, the only human being in a city inhabited by eight million people roaming outside. He started to feel a little nervous, like he shouldn't be here. He hadn't seen a single Jew for a good half hour. Maybe he had left the Jewish sections of Brooklyn. He didn't spot a single mezuzah on any of the doorposts he passed.

He was growing in silent anxiety. He felt a certain pressure in his chest, a bad feeling he couldn't explain. He couldn't go back to the subway station; it was too far away. He was bound to come across another soon; he had seen numerous subway stations dotted throughout the map of the subway. He was too afraid to take it out of his pocket; he didn't want to make any noise. He walked quietly. He could hear the sound of objects moving from dozens of metres away. He would enter the next subway station he found and return to the house immediately.

Something distant confirmed his anxiety, though his feet kept moving, almost as if he no longer had conscious control over them. He heard the sound of a bang. It wasn't close enough to make him jump. He then heard another bang. He was sure they were gunshots. Though he had never heard the sound of gunshots before in real life, he knew these weren't fireworks.

Now filled with more anxiety, and his limbs shaking, he thought to hide behind some dustbins left beside a building in front of him just outside the black gates in front of a house, but a large, black figure ran behind them. Now he jumped as he heard the familiar squeak of a rodent. He saw two more make their way after it. These were rats. These he had seen before.

Now that hiding behind the dustbins was no longer an option, he kept moving, then decided to duck behind a parked car, hoping there were no rats there. He started crying. He could already imagine it. 'Breaking news coming from the BBC of yet another mass shooting in America, this one taking place in Brooklyn on Saturday night, featuring this naïve British national who was stupid enough to travel down the most suspicious parts of New York City late at night on a Saturday.' His face would appear on TV, and his parents would see that their son had died, thus proving them right all along that they had prepared their entire lives full of anxiety for this tragic incident, so that way they wouldn't be too shocked. That way, mourning would be easier, but they'd probably die from a heart attack after finding out the news, anyway.

Simon caught his breath, his limbs still trembling as he wished he could be in one of the houses on this street rather than outside. He imagined knocking on one of the doors to be let in for safety, only for the master of the house to shoot him out of paranoia. He checked around for rats and didn't find any. He didn't know when it would be safe to keep walking so he could flee. Of course, it was his luck that he would find himself in this bloody scene, no pun intended. He took a peep from behind the boot of the car. He saw no one, and he heard no more gunshots. He wiped his tears to confirm more clearly that the streets were empty.

He hunched as he kept walking, and he heard more rats squeaking behind him, near where he had been hiding, which made his back shiver. He looked back several times to make sure no one was there.

After about five more minutes of walking, he found a subway station to his left, though this one was overground. It turned out that he had entered the wrong platform; he should have gone to the other side. He'd transfer later, he thought; all that mattered right now was escaping the area. When he boarded, everyone else in the carriage were sitting down, scrolling on their mobiles. It was nice to see other people again. Little did they know, he thought, that a crime had just taken place nearby.

He never would have guessed how desperate he now was to get back to the Liebermans'. It was the only place he felt safe now in all of America. He wondered how people could live here every day without fear of gun violence. But maybe they did just live with the fear.

He transferred trains and was now underground again. There was only one other person in the carriage, but he didn't care. He was just relieved to be heading in the right direction.

A man came in at one stop, and looked to be mad by his manner of walking, which looked unbalanced. Simon was almost sure he was just about to fall over to his left, then right, then left again as he stumbled. Simon sat by the end of the carriage, whereas the other man on his mobile had been sitting in the centre. The man who had just entered came through the middle doors and looked as though he were about to sit on the same seat as the man.

Simon felt inclined to support the man dressed in a hoodie and coat and stop him from falling over, but he fought hard against this sudden inclination.

His intuition was, once again tonight, correct. The clumsy man started berating the sitting man.

The sitting man didn't even look up, but simply kept scrolling on his mobile, as if this was something he dealt with every day, almost as if he was familiar with this particular man.

Simon's heartrate skyrocketed. He was worried the disoriented man would hit the man sitting down. Seeing that the rogue passenger was only inclined to berate, Simon was worried he was next. He wouldn't be able to handle that. The ride to the next stop seemed to last forever. When the train had finally arrived, he quickly transferred to the adjacent carriage, checking to see if the loud madman would follow, and, thank God, he didn't. He'd then do the same thing and transfer carriages at the next stop, and the one after that, just to stay far away from the man.

He eventually ended up at the Liebermans' house. He couldn't believe what he had been through that night. All the Liebermans had gone to bed. The house was quiet and dark, apart from the kitchen light, which Simon had been asked to turn off upon retiring to the guest room.

Simon changed into his pyjamas feeling restless, yet fatigued. He covered himself in the thick blankets and turned off the lamp on the bedside table, shrouding himself completely in darkness. As the darkness now consumed him, he lay wide-eyed, his heart thumping in his chest as he stared at the ceiling, though his eyes could've been closed; he would've seen no difference. His arms were shaking as he clutched onto the blankets, as if for dear life. His mouth remained open as it suddenly dawned on him: he could've died tonight.

CHAPTER XXIII

When Simon awoke the next morning and recited 'Modeh ani', thanking God for returning his soul into his body, as he did every morning, he had a whole new appreciation for life, dreadful as it was. He kept thinking about his experience last night. He finally got out of bed and went to the kitchen with squinting eyes to do the ritual washing of the hands. Mr and Mrs Lieberman were there, and he was embarrassed to display publicly that he had missed the morning service at synagogue yet again; the digital clock on the oven read half past ten.

'Did you hear about the shootings?' he asked them.

Mrs Lieberman dropped her ladle into the metal pot on the stove, causing it to clang.

'What shooting?'

'There was one in Brooklyn,' said Simon.

'Oh,' she said, attending to her cooking again, as if it weren't a big deal as it hadn't happened in her neighbourhood.

He started shaking. How often did these things happen in America, let alone in New York? He started feeling very unsafe. Mr Lieberman barely seemed to react throughout the exchange. Simon wondered whether he had heard him, or if he was too engrossed in the newspaper lying flat on the kitchen table.

He hoped that Mrs Lieberman wouldn't comment on him having missed the morning service again. He feared he would snap at her. Then he noticed that Mr Lieberman was eating porridge. They must have bought some recently, he thought.

As if on cue, Mrs Lieberman asked him what he'd like for breakfast.

'Some porridge, please,' requested Simon.

'I don't think we have any,' said Mr Lieberman.

'Oh, you've run out?' asked Simon.

He looked at him perplexedly.

Before Mrs Lieberman could respond, Simon pointed at the bowl of porridge sitting on the table by Mr Lieberman.

'You're eating some,' said Simon.

'Oh, *oatmeal*,' said Mr Lieberman, almost as if he were correcting Simon, which somewhat offended him, but he held his tongue. He knew that clarifying cultural differences didn't work so well here; there was one way of doing things and anything else would be taken as an offence.

'We actually have run out,' said Mrs Lieberman, opening a cupboard and seeing that there was none left. She turned to Mr Lieberman. 'Can we buy some more?'

'No, it's OK,' said Simon, not wishing to trouble anyone. 'I'll just take some yoghurt, unless that's called something different in America, too.' Simon genuinely thought this might be a possibility, but he realised after saying this that it could've been taken as an indication of his irritation.

'No, it's called yoghurt here, too,' said Mrs Lieberman, without making eye contact. 'But we pronounce it differently – yoe-gurt.' She handed him some fruit-flavoured yoghurt which had been sitting by Mr Lieberman.

The yoghurt was difficult for Simon to eat. It tasted as though it were fifty per cent sugar, though he would've admitted that there was some sort of fruit somewhere in that mush. He struggled to eat it, then felt sick.

His younger cousins were at yeshiva, so he returned to his bedroom to surf the Internet. He wanted to confirm whether there had been gunshots near where he had been. He came across a news article that reported gunshots heard in the Brooklyn neighbourhood of Bedford-Stuyvesant, which he confirmed through Google Maps was situated just north of Crown Heights. Thankfully, there had been no deaths.

Simon started shaking again. He had been on the periphery of a shooting scene. He then realised that it had been a mistake to come to America. As he reflected in the guest room alone and in silence, he wondered, What am I doing here? What was there to gain? Last night was traumatic, and he felt deeply insecure. He purchased a same-day flight to London. He'd be leaving that night. He hadn't bought a return ticket because he hadn't known how long he would be here; perhaps there was somewhere else he would've liked to travel to in America, but he was done.

Mrs Lieberman said she was sorry to see him go upon hearing he was leaving, but Simon wasn't. His younger cousins seemed a bit sad to say goodbye as well, but Simon was deeply stressed and knew it was the right decision for him.

On the seven-hour flight home, Simon reflected on his experience in America. He thought about The Happy Club, and he couldn't get over what a stupid idea he still thought it was. He intended to live a life of misery in reaction to the concept, and if he was going to be miserable somewhere, he might as well be miserable in a place he was familiar with. He also thought about his experience with the rats and guns – at least it wasn't rats with guns, he thought.

He arrived at Golders Green, and after withdrawing money from his local bank, he realised that after his travels, he had less than two thousand pounds left. He then realised that he'd barely be able to make it through the remainder of his lease with controlled spending, but he couldn't afford to renew it unless he found employment very soon. As he dragged his suitcase to his parents' house, delighted to hear British accents around him again, he thought about possibly staying at his parents' house for some time. He didn't feel comfortable with his housemates avoiding him. He thought he'd stop by his parents' house so he could greet them and they could see he was alive.

'Simon,' said his mother upon greeting him by the door, her face full of shock, 'I didn't expect to see you here so fast!' Indeed, it was Monday afternoon, which meant that Simon had barely been in America for four days.

'Yeah, I missed home,' he said, as if that had been the main reason he had returned, assuming it would be received better than complaining about the gunshots. He dragged his suitcase in and embraced his father, who had come to see who was at the door. 'May I stay here for a little while?'

'Um,' uttered Mrs Jacobs, just as Reuben emerged from the corridor, that familiar person who resembled Simon more than anyone else in the world, as he was also scrawny with brown eyes and straight, brown hair. He would once have contrasted this with being the most unlike him out of anyone in the world regarding their personalities, but Simon now thought that he had become similar to Reuben with his pessimistic approach to things. Perhaps now was an opportune time for a close friendship between the two.

'Oh,' uttered Reuben, clearly not expecting Simon to be there.

Simon then realised that he hadn't notified anyone of his last-minute decision to come back home immediately; his communication with his parents had only consisted of missed calls and voicemails throughout the trip, but it was his parents' house, for God's sake, he thought, and he didn't know why Reuben was making him feel like he wasn't supposed to be there.

'I actually need to talk to you,' said Reuben, looking down at the floor to avoid eye contact.

'Sure,' said Simon, happy to reestablish any communication with his brother.

Mr and Mrs Jacobs appeared delighted to see their sons speaking again, but their smiles vanished and they scattered when they realised they were about to have a serious discussion.

'I don't feel comfortable living in the house anymore,' Reuben told Simon once their parents were out of earshot, 'so I'm going to move in here now. I had meant to tell you, but you were away. I know the lease is under my name, but I was going to put it under yours when it renews in January. I'm in the process of trying to find a replacement.'

'That's funny you mention that,' said Simon, 'because I was thinking about staying here for a while too.'

'Oh,' uttered Reuben, looking somewhat delighted, but then serious again. 'Well, we can't both be living here. In that case, you can take my room or give it to someone else.'

Simon figured he might as well enjoy living in the house he was paying rent for, especially if he probably had about a month left to enjoy it before being unable to pay more rent or renew the lease, but he couldn't renew it and have his name on the lease if he didn't find a job.

'I'll be honest, I haven't got much money,' explained Simon. 'If I don't find a job, I'll be unable to pay rent, assuming I'd be able to fill all the rooms.'

'In that case, I'll keep the lease under my name,' resolved Reuben. 'You can stay there. I'll pay rent for the last month, unless I can still find someone to replace me for a month. If you find a job, I'll put the lease under your name. If you don't, I'll keep it under my name, and we'll find someone else to take your room, and you can move here and the guest room will be yours.'

'OK,' agreed Simon shyly, then realising how much he had been the problem and not the other housemates, he asked, 'Are you angry at me?'

Reuben had turned around to go back to the guest room, but stopped when Simon asked the question. He spoke to him with his back turned, looking down again.

'I'm pretty hurt, but I don't want to talk about that right now,' he said.

'OK,' said Simon.

Reuben returned to the guest room. Simon dragged his suitcase to the corridor, now having to make sure all his belongings were packed and nothing of his had been left in his parents' house as he'd be returning to his own, and he caught sight of Mrs Jacobs there leaning against the wall; she had been listening to the conversation. She straightened up.

'Er, Patrick is sleeping on the bed now,' she said, laughing anxiously.

Simon looked in the bedroom and spotted Patrick napping on the made bed. Indeed, he had already moved on from sleeping under the bed to on top of it.

CHAPTER XXIV

Seeing that all efforts to improve his hopeless life had proved to be in vain, Simon resolved to pass the majority of the day watching TV at home. Every job application had been met with rejection or no response. He would take no risks or do anything that would result in failure, rejection or pain. After the traumatic circumstances he had encountered in America, this was the best sense of progress he could seek.

Reuben was no longer staying at the house now that he was living in their parents' home, and he was actively trying to find a replacement for his room at least for the month of December. Asher and Naphtali were nowhere to be seen, which meant that they were still hiding from Simon or the band was still performing in New York City or somewhere else in America. Either way, Simon enjoyed having the quiet house to himself, though he was heartbroken not to have Patrick around.

On Wednesday, which marked the third day Simon had been back in Britain, Rabbi Isaacs appeared at the afternoon service at synagogue. Simon was delighted to see that he had returned. He wondered when he would see Ezra again. He presumed that Rabbi Isaacs' weekly class on Rashi would resume next Tuesday.

After the evening service was over, half of the congregation had exited when Rabbi Isaacs announced that several of the prayer books and other books had been left around on the tables, and any help returning them to the shelves would be much appreciated.

Simon and only one other volunteer were the only remaining congregants in the synagogue minutes later returning the books. Simon picked up the last three prayer books he could find and brought them to the back bookshelf just next to the way out as the other young man was stuffing prayer books in the small gaps he could find.

The young man, whom Simon recognised as he would show up at synagogue occasionally, took the prayer books from Simon's hands and sorted them.

'Thanks,' said Simon. 'What's your name?'

'Noah. Nice to meet you,' he said, and they shook hands.

Normally, Simon would've returned home to watch TV in the living room, but it was nice to interrupt his daily routine and speak to somebody instead.

They made small talk as they left the synagogue together.

'What do you do?' asked Noah.

Again, that dreadful question, thought Simon. 'I'm actually not working right now,' he muttered.

'Oh, are you looking for a job?' asked Noah.

'I was, but I think I'd like to take a break right now.'

'I understand. I guess sometimes it's better to have no job than work at one you don't like. That would be me.'

'Is it, now?'

'Yes. I'm an accountant. I like the work, but I don't like where I work.'

'Hmm. My brother's an accountant. He seems to enjoy it.'

'My colleagues complain a lot,' complained Noah. 'The clients do, too. I try to stay out of it, but my flatmate complains about a lot of things, too. He also complains about the mess I make, and I complain about his.'

They went down another street. Noah was so negative that Simon felt that he, Simon, and Reuben would make great friends.

'It's so cold,' complained Noah. 'I haven't seen you in a while at synagogue.'

'I was in New York.'

'How was that?'

'Terrible. I'm not kidding when I tell you I was near an actual shooting.'

'Good God. The crime there's serious, and the crime rate here isn't so good, either.'

Finally, someone here who seemed to understand him and how unfortunate life really is, thought Simon.

'I've been there. It's very crowded and expensive,' remarked Noah.

They chatted a bit more until they reached Noah's house.

'We should hang out sometime, maybe grab a coffee,' suggested Noah.

'I'd like that,' said Simon.

Simon smiled as he continued his way back home. It seemed as though he were making a new friend.

CHAPTER XXV

Simon saw Ezra at synagogue that Shabbat. They caught up after the evening service on Friday night and talked more during kiddush after the morning service on Shabbat. Simon was delighted to hear that Ezra wanted to continue their Tea and Torah meetings on Monday. This, coupled with Rabbi Isaacs' Rashi lessons every Tuesday, finally instilled a sense of normalcy in Simon's life. He made meals at home as Reuben was at their parents' house.

After Shabbat ended on Saturday night, he called Noah to ask him if he'd like to join them on Monday night. He declined, stating that he wasn't really interested, though he was still interested in getting together. He suggested going to a local restaurant, but Simon refused as he wanted to cut his spending, but he didn't tell Noah this; he made up an excuse and said he'd just prefer to stay home. So, they settled on Noah coming over for beer on Sunday.

So, that Sunday night, Simon had the TV on and was watching a football match when Noah rang the doorbell.

Noah walked in and Simon handed him a bottle of Heineken, and they sat on one of the living room sofas watching football with a bowl of crisps.

'How are you doing?' asked Simon as the players were getting ready again after the opposing team had scored.

'I'm all right,' said Noah, 'though I've been having some issues with my parents lately.'

Simon swallowed.

'Do you still live with your parents?' asked Simon.

'No, I live in a flat with a flatmate.'

'Oh, right, you've told me,' said Simon.

'I got into an argument with my mum recently,' said Noah, taking a sip of beer. 'I think she can be very negative sometimes.'

Noah then proceeded to speak badly about his parents, which made Simon feel a little uncomfortable, wondering whether he was entitled to hearing such information. Noah would then not speak for nearly fifteen minutes before going on a political rant against the Conservative Party, only to later criticise the Labour Party. In the end, Simon couldn't figure out whether he supported the Tories or Labour. Maybe he was an anarchist.

They spent about two hours watching TV before Noah left. When Simon closed the front door after having seen him out, he couldn't help but realise that he felt much worse after hanging out with Noah than before. He was afraid to admit this to himself because he didn't want to be lonely.

The next day, Ezra came over and the two of them learnt Rashi at the dining table. Simon felt so happy. He couldn't tell whether it was because of the joy of learning Torah or because he was so pleased to be spending time with Ezra again. Perhaps it was both. All he knew was that he hadn't felt this good nor smiled so much for a while.

After the session, Ezra asked him, 'How have you been?'

Simon summarised his trip to America and then said, 'Honestly, life has been hard.'

'How so?'

Simon proceeded to talk about his job search, which hadn't been fruitful, Chaim's abduction, and the awkward situation with Reuben and his friends in The Beis. He suddenly realised how many issues he had, now that he was saying all of this out loud.

'Good God, I'm so sorry to hear all of this,' said Ezra, after listening for nearly half an hour.

'Thank you,' said Simon, who sniffed and shed a tear. He grabbed some tissues from the box on the table and dried his tears. Ezra was the first to hear about his problems all in one go. He had been holding them in after letting them develop these past few weeks because he had no one else to talk to now that Reuben and his old friends didn't talk to him anymore. It felt nice to finally be able to talk to somebody about them.

'Well, it's all coming from Hashem,' pointed out Ezra. 'Our challenges come from God so we can grow. They are tests. You've got an opportunity to work on your faith and trust in God.'

Simon thought about it. He had faith, and he supposed he had some trust. He proceeded to talk about Adam, how he had confronted him after he had been spreading rumours and how all the members of the band had turned against him, it seemed.

'Adam was just a messenger. It's all from Hashem.'

'He could've delivered the message a little more slowly,' said Simon. 'Besides, how am I supposed to trust that this is what is best for me, to lose my friends and have Chaim taken hostage?'

Ezra looked down, nodding.

'I don't know. I can't pretend I have the answers,' he said. 'But think of it this way: are they your true friends if they believe what Adam says and no longer talk to you?'

Simon froze. It was like a wave of truth had crashed against his inner core. He was not prepared for this.

'I guess not.'

Ezra hunched.

'So, it seems like you need new friends! Think about it this way – it's sad what Adam has done, and I'm so sorry to hear you're in this scenario with your friends – but it's like Adam has exposed who your real friends are. True friends would bring up problems with you. Toxic ones would show you no trust or respect. It's not respectful to believe lies told by others, not confront one's friends to clarify things, and then simply not talk to them! Adam has done you a favour!'

Simon kept weeping, grabbing more tissues as he sobbed.

'I'm sorry if I've come off as too strong,' said Ezra.

'No, thank you. I needed to hear that.'

Ezra waited patiently as Simon pulled himself together.

'You seem to have a lot of faith,' observed Simon. 'Where does it all come from?'

'I do have a lot of faith, Baruch Hashem,' said Ezra, which meant 'Thank God'. 'You've just got to work on your relationship with God. You've just got to do whatever it is that brings you closer to Him. For me, it's davening and Torah study,' he said, davening meaning praying.

Simon nodded. He wondered what would bring him closer to God.

'It also helps to have a purpose in life and follow one's goals. It's in *Mesillas Yesharim*, that everyone has a purpose in life.'

Simon thought about it. He didn't know what his particular purpose in life was. He supposed he wanted to raise a family and support them through work, but he was jobless. It then dawned on him that he had never put much thought into what his life's mission was, nor what his goals were.

As this frightening realisation shook him, Ezra continued, 'Well, we had a great session and a good talk. Anything else you'd like to speak about?'

Simon had only revealed the tip of the iceberg, and he had many more questions to ask Ezra, but they'd be talking until Shabbat if he asked them all, so he figured he'd let him go for now.

'No. Thank you so much for listening,' he said, finally feeling some relief from all his troubles.

'My pleasure,' said Ezra, and Simon escorted him out, feeling grateful to have a friend who cared.

CHAPTER XXVI

Simon had immensely enjoyed Rabbi Isaacs' class that week and his session with Ezra, but the silence and emptiness of the house was starting to have a profound impact upon him. The disappearance of his friends had left a significant vacancy in his life, a lack that he felt on a physical level. He had met Noah, but they weren't yet friends. He socialised with Ezra, who was kind, but they hadn't known each other for that long and Simon was not yet inclined to disclose all of his secrets to him. He had been friends with Matthew for years, who had proven his loyalty in the conflict that had arisen with his friends, but he had never approached the level of a confidant. His only sibling, Reuben, had been avoiding him, though he had hinted that reconciliation might be possible at some point in the future. Thus, at the moment, he had no close friends to talk to about personal matters.

That Thursday, towards sunset, he went for a walk. He approached the secondary school he and his friends had attended. It was a fifteen-minute walk from his house. He admired the shadowy edifice, the golden orb of the sun shrouded in part by roaming clouds visible past the school as it was on the verge of setting.

He gazed at the building, which was quiet as the pupils had long been dismissed. He rarely came here. It had been years since he had last done so, and that had been while he was on his way somewhere else. He put his hands in his pockets, gulping as his throat grew sore. His eyes became watery. He reminisced about what seemed now to be simpler days, before Adam had become a member of the friendship group, when everyone had seemed happier and appreciated each other's company much more. Why had Adam had to show up in his life? Couldn't he have stayed in LA?

He sniffed then remembered what Ezra had said. He had shown him who his real friends truly were, but still, their sudden shift in behaviour was so mysterious. He wished he could read their minds.

He recalled memories he had of his friends in the dining hall, in the library, in the gymnasium, but now the sun was setting, and the sky was darkening, and there was no practical reason for staring at the façade of a secondary school for twenty minutes, lest he come across as lost and bizarre to the locals. So, he decided to go home.

On his way there, he saw someone he would've paid not to see, even with the limited amount of money he had left to spend. It was Adam, and he was coming in his direction, just a few metres ahead on the pavement. Adam looked up just after Simon had spotted him. A brief look of fear and surprise appeared on his face before vanishing and becoming serious.

Adam halted just as he was next to Simon, and Simon did the same.

'Oh, Simon,' said Adam, in a way that struck Simon as almost condescending.

Simon wished he were someone else. He wished he weren't speaking to Adam right now. Almost unconsciously, he mentioned the only other person in the world he could have got away with being, saying, 'I'm Reuben.'

'Oh, Reuben,' said Adam, giving a faint, polite smile.

Simon was almost disturbed by the way Adam's facial expression had changed so suddenly. It was like he had become a completely different person with a completely different personality, but then again, it was *he* who was pretending to be a different person. Was Adam fond of Reuben? But now that he was next to a person who had suddenly become hostile towards his real self, he thought to take advantage of this situation. Now that he was operating incognito, he wanted to know what was really going on.

'You know Simon, right?'

'Sure,' said Adam, looking somewhat serious again.

Simon paused, allowing him to elaborate on what he really thought about him, but seeing that he wasn't saying anything else, he now wanted to flow with the pattern of behaviour he had been hearing about.

'Has he been saying anything about me?' asked Simon.

'Not good things,' replied Adam stiffly.

'Like what?'

'He says you're too weak, that you could never learn to play any musical instruments.'

'Did he?'

'Yes.'

'Wow, I can't believe it,' said Simon, faking being hurt. 'Aren't you surprised he would say such a thing?'

'Yes, he seems like a nice guy.'

'Right, thank you,' said Simon, before quickly adding, 'he is a nice guy – well, he seems that way.'

Adam nodded.

'He told me not to tell you, though, but I ought to tell you so you know the truth,' said Adam.

Simon nodded.

'All right, well, thank you for letting me know. See you.'

'See you,' Adam said feebly, a confused look on his face before he kept going.

As Simon ambled down the street, he couldn't believe the exchange he had just had. How could lies be uttered so easily by a human being? He had never come across such evil in his entire life.

He felt so many emotions simultaneously: regret, fear, shock, indignation, anger, sadness, and bitter resentment. He almost felt a little bit of compassion for Adam, because he clearly didn't know a better way to act. Or maybe he did, but he really was that evil.

Also, the band had returned from America, apparently.

Simon felt scared for his friends, knowing now that they were spending time with a compulsive liar. He couldn't believe Adam would utter such lies. He felt so sad that he could lose his friends in such a way, even if it would have been the ultimate test of their friendships.

All of this stress caused him a severe headache. He returned home. Night had fallen, and he was alone. There was no one else around to talk to. Not even his cat.

He went outside and walked over to Ezra's house down the street. He rang the doorbell, and a young man opened the door, looking a bit bewildered by his abrupt appearance.

'Hello, can I help you?' he said.

'Hi, is Ezra here? I'm his friend, Simon.'

'Oh, sure, I'll just go let him know. Please, come in.'

The young man left the front door open and went up the staircase in the dim corridor. Light flowed from the kitchen, barely illuminating the adjacent living room and the rest of the ground floor. All of the housemates must have been relaxing in their bedrooms, unless they had gone out. Ezra's house felt almost as lifeless as his.

Simon stood awkwardly in the living room. He rarely showed up to people's homes without notifying them first, but he was in so much pain tonight. He almost couldn't think straight. He sat down on the sofa in the rather dim living room.

'Oh, Simon,' said Ezra, coming in from the dark corridor. 'My housemate said you were here. Everything all right?'

His housemate appeared by the corridor then left after guessing that Simon was about to disclose personal information.

'It's not,' confessed Simon.

Ezra sat next to him.

'What's wrong?'

'Everything,' said Simon. He sighed, placing the palm of his hand on his forehead, and his head was filled with agony. 'It's Adam. He's spreading lies about me. I don't know what to do.'

Ezra opened his mouth. He looked like he was about to give his answer, but waited for Simon to say what he needed to say.

'No, please speak,' Simon insisted, ready for any advice he could give, even the harshest criticism, as long as it presented the truth, though he couldn't imagine why he would have criticised him as he had done nothing wrong.

'You can only focus on what you can do,' said Ezra. 'It's really sad and messed up, what he's doing, but you can't control other people. You've already spoken to him. He's going to say whatever he wants to say. Your friends will hear what he'll tell them. It's their choice what to do with it.'

'But why is he doing this to me?'

Ezra shrugged.

'I don't know. There could be many reasons, but we may never know. I honestly think you should stop thinking about him. It's only going to bring you more stress.'

'Easier said than done,' said Simon.

CHAPTER XXVII

The next day, as Simon was tidying up the house empty of other housemates in preparation for Shabbat, he thought about the conversation he had had with Ezra last night. He should only focus on what he could control. God would take care of the rest. As he was doing the hoovering in his room, an idea popped into his head. What could he do regarding his friends? He could pretend to be Reuben; he had done so the previous day. Also, the members of the band had apparently come back. He could talk to one of them and instil peace. What would Aharon of the Bible have done to instil peace between people? He would have gone to each one and told them that the other person wished to be reconciled. Couldn't he do the same? He thought it was a brilliant idea.

He turned off the hoover. He doubted anyone in the band would answer his phone call, so he would have to find out where his friends were through Matthew. But who would he approach first? Surely not Dan, who didn't want him to be in the band. He felt too intimidated to approach Yehuda after the recent failed attempt, so he decided on Asher, who used to be nice to him.

He rang Matthew. Shabbat would start within several hours, so Asher was probably at his parents' home preparing for it with his family, seeing that he wasn't here.

Matthew picked up.

'Could you do me another favour, Matthew? Could you check and see where Asher is, but without letting him know I asked you to?'

'Er, sure,' replied Matthew, sounding a bit more uncertain than the last time he'd conducted espionage for Simon.

'Thank you so much,' said Simon. He hung up the phone and waited in his room, wondering how his mission would unfold.

About seven minutes later, Matthew called him back.

'He's by Kosher Kingdom,' reported Matthew.

'Thank you,' Simon said again.

He immediately set off for the supermarket and was kept updated on Asher's location through a series of text messages from Matthew. He felt a bit odd doing this, almost like he was stalking him. He saw him five minutes after passing by the supermarket, waiting to cross a street at a corner.

'Hey, Asher,' he exclaimed, almost forgetting that he needed to pretend to be someone else.

Asher turned around, a concerned look on his face.

'Simon?' he uttered.

'Yeah – no, it's Reuben.'

He stood in front of him, having no other choice than to allow him to analyse him.

'No, you're Simon,' said Asher.

'I'm Reuben,' Simon insisted.

Asher hesitated, and then said, 'You're Simon. I can tell by your voice. And only Simon would wear that jacket,' he said, almost sneering at his black jacket.

This was true; it was Simon's jacket. Reuben wore a blue one. He wondered whether Asher secretly held something against his fashion sense. Still, he didn't want to give up so easily. It would've pained him to see him go with that. So, he changed his voice to sound a bit softer, like Reuben's.

'It's me, Reuben.'

'Don't lie to me, Simon,' snapped Asher. Simon now wished he hadn't done this; he had never aggravated Asher this much before. 'I need to go.'

And with that, he left, crossing the street.

As he left, Simon had no choice but to return home. Later, he remembered that his friends didn't like Reuben and had even requested Simon stop including him in their plans. Now he was starting to wonder how it would've gone with Asher had he just been himself. Should he try again? He was feeling desperate now. It made him feel pathetic. He felt hopeless again; nothing was working.

CHAPTER XXVIII

Simon couldn't help but perceive the difference in the way he felt when he had spent time with Noah and with Ezra. Noah left him feeling empty and hopeless, whereas Ezra left him feeling excited about life, inspired and optimistic. Nevertheless, Noah asked if he could come over again Sunday night to have a beer and watch sports, and Simon accepted.

But before that, Simon decided to go to Epping Forest. He took Ezra's advice to do whatever he could to come closer to God, and the first thing he thought of was to spend time in nature.

There, gazed at all the trees and the blue sky and the clouds overhead. He looked at all the plants, and he thought to himself: every tree, every animal, every rock that I see was created by Hashem. He marvelled at this idea, and at the world around him.

He took inspiration from the animals. If they were able to live without worry, with Hashem providing them with their every need, how much more so should Simon, who knew this on a conscious level and had been taught about the concept of bitachon, or trust in God?

The application of Ezra's advice was working well. Simon remembered how Ezra had spoken of gratitude, how in *Pirkei Avot*, one who was rich was one who was happy with his lot. Was Simon happy? He was grateful that his parents were alive and well, as well as Reuben, and his mother had told him that his grandmother had recovered from Covid, which meant that all his grandparents were alive and well. He had a house to live in. Sure, he was facing the possibility of having to move out due to being unable to pay rent, but his parents would have easily taken him in. Sure, he had no job, but he was a healthy, fit twenty-four-year-old who was capable of working at a new job.

Suddenly, his mood shifted. Amidst the greenery, he started remembering lessons he had learnt at yeshiva, things he had learnt with Ezra, in Rabbi Isaacs' lessons, and things he knew intuitively. He was starting to feel a little happier. He had a lot to be grateful for. After about an hour and a half of walking around, he felt he was ready to go home.

He was not looking forward to spending time with Noah, feeling that he would probably be a burden to him. As he headed back to Golders Green, he thought that maybe Noah wasn't perennially miserable, but Simon just happened to have spent time with him during some of his moody spells.

But he was wrong. Noah came over that night, and their hang-out was not much different from the last. They drank some beer and watched football, which felt nice, but Noah would constantly criticise the players of both teams. Even when their team scored, Noah would point out how if the previous failed passes had not occurred, the goal would've been scored a lot more quickly. Winning the match didn't seem to make a difference to Noah's mood. He criticised everything, from the weather to politics. He was complaining about how his porridge that morning had come out burnt when Simon lied and said that he was feeling tired and it was his bedtime and saw him out, only to realise after looking at the digital clock on the oven that it was only a quarter to nine.

Simon came to the painful realisation that he didn't enjoy his time spent with Noah at all and didn't want to be friends with him. Noah seemed to sympathise with Simon when he spoke about his problems or his more negative viewpoints on life, but he only seemed to remain in the realm of pessimism. Simon felt he appreciated nothing and his disposition was inclined to seek that which he didn't like about life, or what was going wrong, but without doing anything about it.

Simon wondered how he'd go about cooling things between them. They had only been hanging out for a couple of weeks. It wasn't like they had been best friends for years. He figured he would simply stop hanging out with him. He would make small talk if they saw each other at synagogue, but if Noah continued to initiate hanging out, he would have to break the news to him. He hoped Noah would get the hint before it reached that point.

CHAPTER XXIX

'So,' said Ezra during their next learning session, 'life isn't just about what you take, but what you get – I mean, give.'

Simon nodded. He thought about it. What did he have to give to the world?

He quite enjoyed his weekly learning sessions with Ezra. They would learn for an hour and then they'd talk about their personal lives. It always left Simon feeling inspired, understood, and overall happier.

When Simon told him again about his personal struggles, including how sad he was that his friends would no longer speak to him, Ezra reminded him, 'You have to focus on what you can control. You can't dwell on how they're behaving or how you can change them to get them to do what you want them to do. To change someone else is impossible. To change yourself takes a miracle. You have to decide how you're going to respond to this situation because that's all you can do. So, what are you going to do?'

Simon nodded, thinking about it. He told him about pretending to be Reuben in front of Adam, and how he had done the same thing to Asher, and how fruitless the results were. Ezra remained silent. Simon realised that he hadn't answered his question.

'Make new friends,' he concluded.

'I know life can be hard,' said Ezra. 'And we can talk about emunah and bitachon,' emunah meaning faith, 'but it all boils down to whether you truly believe things could get better, and whether you're capable of success. The human will, or ratzon, is strong. Will you desire for your life to get better? Will you strive to improve your life? Will you focus on the positive in life and not dwell on the negative without making any changes? It's up to you!'

Simon took in his words and reflected on them. He was speechless. Could he change his life with determination? It seemed like such a heavy responsibility. It filled him with anxiety, even though it was inherently empowering.

'I, for one, think you're capable,' said Ezra.

'Thank you,' said Simon, smiling. He then realised that Ezra was a positive influence in his life, that he admired and cared about him, and that he would've liked and could benefit a lot from spending more time with him. They only had a weekly commitment and didn't spend much time together, apart from when they'd see each other in synagogue. 'Feel free to come over any time.'

'Sure, that sounds great,' said Ezra.

Ezra left shortly afterwards. Simon was grateful to have him living so close to him. He realised that Hashem had put him there so they could eventually become friends. He was happy to have a positive influence nearby.

That night, he thought some more about what Ezra had said. Was he determined to improve his life situation? Did he believe he was capable? He did want things to get better. He recognised the value of living a happy life with optimism. It felt good. It helped him be kinder to others. He functioned better mentally, and he could serve Hashem more easily. He knew this because he was happier after spending time with Ezra. He felt bad that Reuben didn't seem to practise this way of thinking and living, and he had no ambition to start his own Happy Club, nor did he think it worthwhile to strive for unrealistic, impractical and baseless optimism, but he was willing to look at the more positive side of things. It was clear to him that he needed to keep Adam out of his life and Ezra in.

That night, he cried into his pillow and prayed, asking God for help. He wanted things to get better. He had to focus on what he could control. He couldn't control his friends. He couldn't dispel the false rumours. He couldn't release Chaim from Hamas, assuming he was still alive, nor could he know whether he was alive.

There were many things he couldn't control. Yet, all that Hashem did was for his best. If so, maybe he was mislabelling his life and all its occurrences as bad. Was it bad that he was without a job? Was it bad that his friends had betrayed him by disappearing? How was his life good?

For one, he had a study partner, a chavrusa, Ezra, who seemed trustworthy. Was he going to betray him, too? He couldn't control that, he remembered. What he could control, however, was praying. He beseeched Hashem that Chaim would be released, because that was what he could do. He was determined to figure out what his raison d'être was.

The whole week was marked by intense anxiety and trepidation. A deal had been reached with Hamas in which they would be releasing select hostages. Every day, Simon anxiously checked for updates to see whether Chaim had been released. It seemed as though most were women and children and foreign nationals, so it appeared unlikely that Chaim would be one of them, but he stubbornly kept praying for Chaim. He found it difficult to pay attention during Rabbi Isaacs' class on Tuesday night, which had previously been a source of relief and serenity. Throughout the class, he constantly fought the urge to excuse himself and go on his mobile to read more updates.

On Wednesday, Simon saw a picture of Chaim amongst those who had been released that day. He couldn't believe his eyes. He reread the post, making sure he really had been among those released and not – God forbid – murdered, before he would celebrate. Indeed, he had been released.

He jumped in ecstasy. He hadn't expected this to happen, although deep down he had hoped for it. Tears poured down his cheeks uncontrollably as he called Chaim, but he didn't pick up. He cleared his throat as he called his mother, who picked up and confirmed while also weeping that Chaim had been returned and was home. Simon then wondered how much trauma and suffering he had endured, and – God forbid – if he had gone through any torture.

'May I speak with him?' asked Simon.

'He's sleeping now,' said Mrs Spiegel.

Simon accepted this. Chaim being alive was all he wanted to hear. It truly felt like a miracle. He could easily wait a week if he had to. As long as Chaim was alive and well, he could be at peace. He felt as if he could be happy and grateful to God forever, as if he had no right to complain about anything ever again. His friend was alive.

It was then that he faintly heard footsteps coming from downstairs, and at least two people conversing. He hung up after speaking with Chaim's parents.

He accepted that his friends from The Beis were no longer his friends; no one had made the effort to contact him. Asher and Naphtali wouldn't speak to him, presumably due to Adam's rumours, and he had tried calling Yehuda, but he hadn't responded. Though he would've normally been angry at Adam for having caused this, he was thankful that he had exposed who his real friends truly were. His gentle approach regarding his distancing from Noah also seemed to have worked; they didn't hang out anymore and Noah hadn't tried to initiate any more get-togethers; they'd only engage in polite small talk at synagogue. Noah seemed to enjoy this. Maybe Simon's increasingly positive demeanour was inspiring Noah to change his ways too.

Simon went downstairs, wondering who had been there, but he saw no one. Then he noticed that Asher's and Naphtali's belongings were all gone.

CHAPTER XXX

That Shabbat, Simon had quiet meals at home yet again as Reuben ate at their parents' house. He had managed to do a bit of cleaning before Shabbat came, but most of the mess was still there. Before his learning sessions with Ezra, he would simply clear the dining table of dishware and silverware only to leave them in the kitchen sink unwashed for days, and he would reorganise the mess in the living room only to pile everything up in a corner, yet to be sorted properly.

That Sunday, Simon had an hour-long conversation over the phone with Chaim. Thank God, he was doing OK. He was understandably traumatised. In the middle of the conversation, Simon couldn't help but weep. He remained silent as he did so, covering his mouth to prevent the sound of sobbing from coming out. He didn't want to overwhelm him with his own emotions. It seemed as though Chaim couldn't believe that he was alive either.

'Idan is in Gaza, fighting,' said Chaim, his voice a bit softer than usual. Simon wondered if he felt weak. He had to turn the volume up on his mobile and press his ear against the speaker in order to hear him properly. He would also take longer pauses than usual between phrases. 'I haven't seen him since I came back. How is your brother?'

'He's well. We're still not talking as much,' answered Simon.

'You should talk to him,' said Chaim.

Simon couldn't help but recognise the truth in that simple solution. He figured he'd try to initiate a conversation with Reuben. After he finished his conversation with Chaim, he thanked God and was filled with gratitude as Chaim was back at his home in Jerusalem.

About an hour later, Reuben arrived. Simon greeted him at the door, but they didn't talk much.

Reuben walked around in the living room before passing through the house and stopping by the back door. He put his hands on his sides. He appeared to stare absent-mindedly at the garden, before becoming aware once again of the physical world around him.

'The garden is full of weeds,' he observed.

'Right. I had meant to weed it,' said Simon.

Reuben returned to the living room, mercifully ignoring the mess there; perhaps he was more focused on his thoughts again. He sighed. Simon wondered whether it was something about him. He was preparing himself to dispel any rubbish Adam had told him.

'Asher and Naphtali have moved out,' Reuben said.

'I know,' uttered Simon.

'They've paid the last month's rent, which I appreciate,' continued Reuben. 'They may try to find replacements, but I'm going to try to find some, too. It's already December.'

Reuben collapsed onto the sofa. He laid his head back and shut his eyes.

'What is it?' asked Simon.

'I'm just worried about finding replacements,' said Reuben as his eyes remained shut. 'I won't be able to manage for so long if it's just us after a few months.'

Just us, Simon repeated in his mind. Did this mean that he was open to living in the same house together again?

Simon and Reuben remained in their positions, with Reuben sitting and Simon standing in silence for almost a full minute, then Simon fetched his guitar from his bedroom. He dusted it, tuned it, and played the song 'God Put a Smile Upon Your Face' by Coldplay, singing it also.

He noticed Reuben open his eyes and a more hopeful expression appeared on his face.

Next, he played and sang 'Yesterday' by The Beatles.

When he was finished, Reuben said, 'Thank you.'

'Are you angry at me?' Simon asked.

'No,' replied Reuben.

'It wasn't anything Adam said?'

'What?' asked Reuben, now looking at him perplexedly.

Simon paused.

'Did Adam tell you anything about –'

He paused again. Reuben looked utterly bewildered.

'What are you talking about?' asked Reuben.

'Nothing,' said Simon. 'I just get the sense you're speaking to me less. If it's something I've done or said, please tell me.'

Reuben sat silently for a moment, then said, 'I've been a bit hurt by some of the things you've done.'

Simon was shocked, trying to recall anything he had done that would have vexed Reuben. Surely this was something to do with Adam spreading lies again.

'What?'

'Some of it I have got over,' admitted Reuben. 'Like when you said you didn't want me hanging out with you and your friends anymore.'

'I don't mind hanging out with you,' clarified Simon. He then realised it was unlikely that it could have been related to anything Adam might have told him, because Reuben had long been excluded from the group to begin with.

'I thought about it,' continued Reuben, nodding. 'I understand it was your friends' wishes, not yours, and I understand the reasons why, and it's something I'm trying to work on. I'm working on being more social. But I was upset by the way you were yelling at me about leaving a mess around. I know I could be cleaner, but I didn't like the way you were treating me.'

Simon then recalled the boisterous way in which he had confronted Reuben about this issue.

'Oh, you're right. I'm so sorry,' said Simon. 'I didn't mean to be so hard on you. Please forgive me. I was going through a lot. I'm not excusing my behaviour for that, but I will try to be more mindful of how I speak to you. I didn't mean to hurt you.'

Reuben nodded.

'I forgive you. Sorry for not talking as much. I wasn't sure how to approach the subject.'

'That's quite all right,' said Simon, suddenly realising that he and Reuben had not had much experience resolving their conflicts because they hadn't really had any major ones. They had always seen eye to eye. Simon was glad to have Reuben's support again. He had been a constant source of security and loyalty. Up until now, he hadn't realised how much he had been taking him for granted.

Reuben made eye contact with him and smiled.

'Are you still going through those issues?' asked Reuben.

'Well, not so much,' said Simon. 'Those friends you were talking about, well, we're not so much friends anymore.'

It was then that Simon remembered that time he had pretended to be him during his interaction with Adam. Little did Reuben know that someone from the group had thought that he had been interacting with him.

'Sorry to hear that,' said Reuben. 'Well, Hashem puts people in our lives for a reason. We may not always know the reason.'

'What do you mean?' asked Simon, not knowing why God had placed his friends in his life and kept them in it for so many years only to take them away. He felt as though God had been teasing him.

'Hashem puts people in your life for a reason,' explained Reuben. 'Everything He does is for a reason. There's a reason why He made me brothers with you.'

Simon wondered why Hashem had made him brothers with Reuben, and why He had made him his twin on top of that, always having to share the same birthday.

Nonetheless, he kept playing the guitar. Reuben started humming along to the melodies.

'Thanks for the music,' said Reuben. 'It made me feel a lot better.'

After hearing these words and seeing the smile on Reuben's face, a rush of excitement ran through Simon's body. There was something transcendental, almost euphoric that Simon felt, knowing he had helped someone through the power of music.

It was then when Simon recognised what his purpose in life was: to make people feel better through music. For so long, he had enjoyed playing music, composing music, and sharing it with others. He felt joyous and relieved to have finally discovered his mission in life. He finally felt he had direction. He knew what he needed to do: form a band, make music, and perform for others.

The only question was: who would join? He knew the members of The Beis were no longer an option. He would have to find his own musicians somehow.

CHAPTER XXXI

'I'm sorry,' said Ezra after their next Tea and Torah session, which once again only included the two of them, 'but I don't really play any musical instruments.'

Simon would've loved for Ezra to be a part of his band, but he acquiesced. Just because they were good friends didn't mean that they had to form a professional relationship.

Reuben moved back into the house. Simon assumed it was due to their having made peace. It was nice to have the whole house just to themselves, though of course they both had on their minds the need to seek replacements for Asher's and Naphtali's old rooms.

Simon spent the next few days weeding the garden and cleaning up the mess in the house. He had found mould growing in several areas and had to deal with that. All the houseplants were long dead; it was not a matter of saving them but a question of whether to replace them. He went to the local garden centre and purchased a few new indoor plants, keeping in mind his dwindling finances, which he placed in the kitchen and living room. He also retrieved Patrick from his parents' house now that he seemed responsible enough to take care of him again. Upon retrieving him, he found him asleep on the bed in the guest room. It seemed as though his parents' house had been growing on Patrick as he appeared reluctant to be put into his cage and relocate again, but he quickly made himself at home in Simon's house and returned to Simon's bedroom, where he'd normally spend most of the day. Simon was so happy to have Patrick home again. By Wednesday, half the garden was free of weeds. It looked as though it were a weed farm, and Simon had just harvested half the field.

Once his chores were taken care of, he remembered that Chanukah was starting this week and anxiously grabbed his silver menorah from the cupboard, opened the curtain in the living room and stationed the menorah on a table by the window. He said the appropriate blessings and kindled the wick for the first night, then said 'Maoz Tzur' to himself. He would've loved to sing it with Reuben, but he had been anxious to welcome Chanukah into the house. He also wasn't sure when Reuben would be arriving, and he could always sing with him when he lit his menorah later.

Someone knocked on the door. Simon only expected Reuben, but he had a key to the house. Could it be Matthew?

He opened the door and saw that it was Dan. He froze. What was he doing here?

Dan smiled.

'Hello, Simon. May I come in?'

'Sure,' uttered Simon, stepping aside so Dan could hang his coat on the rack and stuff his gloves into his coat pockets.

Simon was utterly confused. They hadn't spoken in weeks. Why was Dan acting as though nothing had happened? He was expecting an apology.

'How are you?' asked Dan.

'Great,' said Simon in a flat tone.

Dan nodded, then spotted the lit menorah in the living room.

'Mate, it's not Chanukah yet,' said Dan.

'What?'

'Chanukah starts tomorrow night.'

'Oh,' said Simon, rushing to extinguish the flames. He couldn't believe he had kindled the menorah a night too early. He felt terrible. He had uttered Hashem's name in vain. Then, he stopped his negative train of thought. Normally, he'd remain in despair and suffer from guilt, but he had made a mistake. He would be more careful in future about making sure when the holidays started. There wasn't a Jewish calendar in the house. Perhaps he'd buy one. He would apologise to Hashem once Dan had gone.

'I haven't seen you in a while,' said Simon.

'Yeah, I feel bad,' said Dan, looking down at his shoes. 'I'm very sorry. I've just been so busy.'

'It's OK,' said Simon, wondering how sincere Dan was being.

'What have you been up to lately?' asked Dan.

'I've been trying to start my own band,' said Simon.

'Ah, is that so? Could I be in it?'

'You've got enough time to be in two?' asked Simon.

Dan shrugged. 'I could try.'

Then someone opened the door. Reuben appeared, taking off his coat and removing his scarf.

'Hi,' he said, sneering at Dan.

Simon didn't expect Dan to stay much longer. He knew this had become an awkward moment. Reuben lived here and Dan had been one of the pioneers in not allowing Reuben to hang out with the group. As expected, Dan left shortly afterwards.

'I see you've prepared for Chanukah,' said Reuben after Dan had left.

Simon looked at the menorah. Two of the cups had been filled with olive oil and carried ashy wicks.

'I have,' replied Simon.

'I've been trying to make my own friends,' said Reuben as he switched the kettle on in the kitchen. 'It's quite hard, though.'

Simon wanted to tell Reuben that he was delightful just the way he was, but he wanted him to be able to make good friends on his own, so he would save his praise for when he'd been successful in this endeavour.

He then thought about his old friends. Was Dan's visit the start of a new trend? Would Yehuda want to speak to him again too? Had they come to realise that he'd actually been a good friend and Adam's rumours had been mostly lies, that he'd meant no harm?

CHAPTER XXXII

Over the next few days, Simon finished weeding the garden. With Reuben's help, the whole house was now spotless. The two brothers spent Shabbat meals together at their parents' house. Simon was wondering who would be in his band, and how he could meet potential players. Reuben didn't play any instruments, but Simon spread the word to his family and Ezra that he was actively seeking musicians.

That Sunday, Matthew called and asked if he could come over, and Simon made them some tea. He hadn't thought of asking Matthew to join the band he intended to form, but he thought to bring it up at some point during their meeting.

They sat down and conversed in the living room. Reuben was out and Patrick was on Simon's bed, sleeping.

'This may come as a bit of a surprise,' said Matthew, before taking a sip of warm tea, 'but Adam asked me to decide whether I should be friends with you or him, essentially.'

'What?' exclaimed Simon, not having expected to hear Adam's name again.

'I'm not sure if you've heard,' said Matthew, 'but the band broke up.'

'What?' repeated Simon, his world seemingly flipping upside down.

'Yeah. Adam seems upset. But he basically told me – almost as if he were speaking for the whole group – that I need to decide whether I'll keep talking to you, or else he couldn't associate with me anymore.'

'Are you joking?' said Simon, wondering how much drama could develop regarding him without him even communicating with those involved. This only confirmed his decision not to speak to Adam anymore.

'I'm afraid not,' said Matthew. Then, he shrugged. 'So, I don't speak to him anymore. It wasn't a difficult choice to make. The other members of the band don't speak to me anymore, either. It's a bit weird. It's like he's got them on a leash. But this happened a while before, before the band broke up. I just decided to let you know now.'

'When did the band break up?' asked Simon.

'A week or two ago,' answered Matthew.

'Why?'

'I don't know,' replied Matthew. 'Honestly, I don't speak to them much anymore.'

Simon couldn't believe it. He and Matthew were now in the same boat regarding where they stood with the others. This news also gave a different nuance to his situation regarding Dan, with regard to both his apology and his request to be a part of Simon's band. The Beis had been dissolved. Was Dan sincere about reconnecting with Simon and starting a band, or had he realised he had no other option after his had ended and was now simply band-hopping? Simon didn't know whether he could trust Dan, but he knew where he stood with Matthew.

'I'm trying to start my own band,' said Simon. 'Would you like to be part of it?'

Matthew grinned. Simon knew that the two of them were sort of rejects of Adam's band, Simon against his will and Matthew through conscious choice, and this idea felt rather empowering to the both of them.

'I'd love to,' said Matthew.

Simon felt overjoyed by this unequivocal enthusiasm.

'Great!' he said. 'We've got an acoustic guitar player and a bassist.'

'I've also got a friend, Henry,' said Matthew. 'He's great at drums. May I ask him whether he'd like to join?'

'Of course,' said Simon. He was delighted that a potential band member would be coming through a trustworthy source. He was a bit surprised by how quickly he was finding musicians – three prospective players!

'Great. I'll try to arrange a meeting,' said Matthew. 'Just one thing: I've got a day job. Would you mind if we keep this as a sort of side project?'

Simon accepted the condition.

CHAPTER XXXIII

Simon was hoping to avoid the question as to whether Dan should be let into the band. He hoped he would find a singer so he wouldn't have to address the issue. He knew, however, that Dan had an assertive personality, maybe bordering on aggressive at times. He knew he'd be following up again and again until he received a 'yes' or 'no'.

Which was why Simon wasn't surprised when Dan rang him on Monday. He ignored the phone call. At the time, he was preparing a festive meal. Tonight would be the fifth night of Chanukah. Along with his regular Tea and Torah session with Ezra, he planned to have a small gathering with food and celebration. Matthew would be bringing his friend Henry Ward.

Simon and Ezra had a half-hour study session with Reuben present. Just as they'd concluded the session, someone knocked on the door.

'Coming!' Simon called out.

He opened the door and there were Matthew and Henry. Simon shook hands with Henry.

'Pleasure to meet you,' he said.

'Thanks for having me,' said Henry.

'I hear you play drums?' said Simon as they came in and hung up their coats, the chilly December air sweeping into the house until Simon shut the door.

'Yes. I hear you're starting a band?' replied Henry.

'I am,' Simon said.

'I'd love to join. Would you like me to show you my drumming skills sometime?'

'No, that's fine. If Matthew recommended you, I'll take his word for it.'

'Wonderful,' said Henry as they entered the dining room. 'So, how many members are we?'

'So far, there's just the three of us,' said Simon. 'I only recently came up with the idea. I'll have to play you some songs I've written. I'd love to see how you can accompany them on the drums.'

'Great,' said Henry.

Simon and Reuben brought out the dishes and serving utensils.

As Simon laid a serving platter full of golden latkes on the dining table, he received a phone call. He took out his mobile as the others engaged in conversation.

It was Dan. He froze. It was like his past and present worlds were colliding. He swallowed as he silenced his mobile. This time, Dan left a voicemail. He was anxious to know what message it contained, but he had to leave it for later. He wanted to enjoy the moment.

'Henry, have you ever been to a Chanukah event before?' he asked as he sat down and finally began eating.

'I haven't,' answered Henry, who, like his friend Matthew, wasn't Jewish, 'but I do see Jews lighting menorahs on their windowsills. I see you've got some here on a table. You've got two.'

Indeed, Simon and Reuben had placed their kindled menorahs on a small table by the window, which gave light to the dark living room, which contrasted with the bright dining room.

'Yes, we both have to light our own menorahs, Reuben and I.'

'Simon,' said Ezra, 'I forgot to tell you. A very friendly man at synagogue invited me to come for a meal Friday night for Shabbat. He said I could bring a friend. Would you like to come?'

'Sure,' answered Simon. He enjoyed the meals with Reuben at home or at his parents' house, but a break from the routine was most welcome.

The meal continued, and they spoke about the meaning behind Chanukah and some of the reasons why there were eight nights of Chanukah and not seven, when the oil in the Temple lasted for seven extra days and not eight.

Later, Reuben mentioned to Simon, 'Asher found somebody to take his room. I thought that was very considerate of him. His name is Levy. He should be moving in tomorrow.'

'Oh, great,' said Simon. He then felt a little low after the mention of Asher's name. He thought about his old friends. He wondered what went on in their minds, if they ever thought of him, if they ever secretly wished to speak to him.

Now that The Beis had disbanded, they were presumably no longer under Adam's negative influence, unless they still socialised with him. If not, surely they would have gathered their wits and would wish to speak to him again.

Then, someone knocked on the door. As Simon approached it, passing through the dark living room, he wondered who it could be. He opened it and saw that it was Dan. He instantly knew that it had been a mistake not to have answered the call and told Dan – or at least texted him – that he was busy and would get back to him later.

'Hey, I was worried about you. I called you and you didn't pick up. You usually answer right away, so I just wanted to pass by and see whether you were all right,' said Dan, looking a bit anxious.

'I'm fine,' said Simon. He stood in the doorway because he didn't want Dan mingling with everyone else – Dan wasn't too fond of Reuben anyway, so in a way he was doing him a favour – because he hadn't invited Dan and because he was no longer sure whether he could trust him after his band had broken up. He hoped he wouldn't hear everyone else chatting in the dining room, but then Matthew cracked a joke, and the others laughed audibly.

Dan looked past him in the direction of the noise, then looked back at Simon.

'Can I talk to you?' Dan asked.

Simon sighed.

'Sure. Let's go for a walk.'

Simon grabbed his coat. He felt bad to miss out on the fun with everyone else, but he planned to excuse himself should the walk start to seem as if it was going to take too long. He wondered what important words Dan had to share with him. He wrapped his scarf around his neck and put on his hat, then set off into the cold December night with Dan. After having a quick word with him, he planned to return to the party without him.

'What is it?' he asked Dan as they walked down his street.

'Have you decided whether I could be part of your band?' asked Dan.

'No, I haven't.'

'Why not?'

'I'm still going over the practicalities of what I'd like my band to be. It may take some time.'

'Oh.'

But Simon didn't want to let him go there. As they turned right onto Golders Green Road, he said, 'I heard The Beis broke up.'

'Yes,' admitted Dan, 'that was just horrible, a horrible time.'

Simon pricked up his ears.

'Are you sad about it?' he asked.

'I mean,' said Dan, 'it was a horrible experience. I'm actually quite relieved it's over. Honestly, it was just before the end that was the worst.'

'How so?' asked Simon, relishing the insight.

'Adam was becoming quite toxic. It was his idea to go to New York because his team suggested we go there. He said we were going to play at big Jewish and secular venues. Well, we were there for two weeks and we played at two events, both of them small, and I still had to pay for everything, from food to flight tickets to my share of the taxi rides. It was terrible. He made us rehearse for hours every day. He even made us rehearse on Motzei Shabbat,' he complained, meaning Saturday night after Shabbat was over. 'His team apparently networked through Facebook.'

'What team?' asked Simon.

'I don't know, mate. He says he works with a team who networks and advertises for us. I've never met them. I don't even think he has one.'

'So, what made you guys break up? Weren't you performing at a few venues here?'

'We did some venues here in London, yes,' he said, 'but they were all small. He was promising we'd do big events, weddings, but that just never happened. We've spent so many weeks rehearsing endlessly, and we've actually performed at maybe six events? Most were small and informal.'

'So, what made you guys break up?'

'I think Yehuda was the first. He got into an argument with him in America. Then they argued again after we came back. He was threatening to leave, and that was when Adam decided it was a negative environment and that he couldn't manage the band anymore. The rest of us were a bit shocked. Sure, we were upset and had our disagreements, but we relied on Adam for everything and he had really taken the lead, so once he announced the band was over, we kind of took his word for it and never played together again.'

'Do you still see each other?'

'I don't see Adam anymore, but the others, yes.'

'Do they say anything about me?'

'I honestly think Yehuda feels very sorry about not getting back to you, but honestly, we're all so tired and stressed after everything that went on.'

'What about Asher and Naphtali?'

'I don't see them much, but they haven't really said anything about you. Honestly, we're just tired and shocked.'

Simon had stopped on the pavement to take all this in.

He thought about it. Dan had betrayed his trust by not having spoken up for him when he had tried to join his former band, even if it had clearly worked out for the best. He had also apologised, but this was Simon's project and he wasn't going to take any chances this time around. He could forgive Dan, and maybe even be friends again, but he had made his decision, and he would not let him into the band.

'I'm sorry, Dan, but I'm going to pass on your offer to join my band.'

'What? Why?' asked Dan, looking genuinely shocked.

Simon had feared the question. He didn't know how to explain it to him nicely, and he knew he was going through a lot. He settled on being tactful, but honest.

'I cannot let you be a part of it after everything we've been through. I hope you understand.'

Dan looked down and nodded, which caused a pain in Simon's chest.

'I understand,' Dan acquiesced.

Simon felt bad, but he also felt relieved that he had finally expressed to Dan how he truly felt, and that he had accepted the sentiment.

CHAPTER XXXIV

The next day, Simon was playing the instrumental accompaniment to his song 'Candles' on his guitar as he sat on his bed. He had rehearsed it earlier that day as he planned to show it to the new members of his band. He then heard someone playing the electric guitar downstairs. He started. Was Asher here?

He braced himself for their encounter, though he noticed as he stood by his bedroom door that he was playing a lot softer and more slowly than usual. Perhaps it was someone else. It would be very uncharacteristic of Asher to play here after popping in, but stranger things had occurred in his life.

As he descended the steps, he discovered a stranger playing the electric guitar in the living room. He was Simon's height, with tan skin and short, dark hair. He looked up at Simon as he descended the stairs and smiled while continuing to play.

Simon then remembered his new housemate would be moving in today. The rucksack lying on the sofa suggested he had brought his possessions to move in. He then noticed a suitcase by the back door.

'Hi,' he said, shaking hands with Simon. 'I'm Levy Silverstein, a friend of Asher's.'

Simon swallowed at the sound of Asher's name. He wondered if Asher had told him anything bad about him. Who knew what rumours could have been circulating.

'Welcome,' said Simon.

'Right, I still need to bring my suitcase up. I was just admiring the garden.'

Simon nodded, remembering how messy it had been not too long ago. He thought about his band, and how he could use an electric guitar player. By the way he played, he'd accept him into the band right away. He just had to know whether he was available. He was excited by the prospect of having a fourth member of the band.

'I see you play very well,' remarked Simon.

'Oh, cheers. I used to jam with Asher a lot, especially when we were in yeshiva together.'

'How is Asher doing?'

'Pretty well. We don't talk as much as we used to. He seemed pretty stressed after his band broke up. I'm sure you've heard.'

'I have. How did you hear about this house?'

'I'd actually made Asher aware a while ago that I was looking for a flat. He mentioned the room and the rent and I thought it was a good deal.'

Simon wanted to ask Levy whether Asher had said anything negative about him. But then, he let it go. Levy probably wouldn't have moved in here if he had had a reason not to trust someone who lived here. He also didn't want to come across as suspicious. He was hoping that his social interactions from here on would be free from such dramatic energy.

'I'm actually trying to start a band,' said Simon. 'Not a full time thing, it's more of a side project. Would you be interested in joining?'

He never would have guessed he'd be asking someone to join the band within fifteen minutes of meeting him, but he liked the way he played, he was anxious to start it, and they were now housemates. He did, however, think it a bit weird that it was a mutual friend of his and Asher's.

'Sure, I would,' said Levy.

Simon was taken aback by this affirmation.

'Brilliant!' he exclaimed.

And so, Levy Silverstein became the fourth member to join Simon's band.

That night, Simon, Matthew, Henry, and Levy gathered in the living room for a jam session. Simon played the acoustic guitar accompaniment to his song 'Candles' for them, which felt timely as it was still Chanukah. They nodded and smiled as he demonstrated the concept. He found it a bit difficult to play the guitar and sing the lyrics simultaneously. There was a point when Levy tried to play chords on his electric guitar to support him, but he had trouble following Simon's harmonic progression, and he gave up. Simon sang the rest of the song without any musical accompaniment.

They all clapped.

Simon was surprised by their approval. Adam had hated it.

'Bravo,' said Henry. 'You wrote that?'

'I did,' answered Simon, his words struggling to pass through his throat. He was getting emotional with all the sudden acknowledgement.

'That was brilliant,' said Levy.

'Very good,' said Matthew, who had heard it before.

Simon then played it again so they could improvise an accompaniment to it. Henry was brilliant on the drums. Levy harmonised well with his electric guitar while Matthew played the bass guitar. It all sounded so wonderful, and this was their first jamming session. Simon sang and played his guitar when he could. He hadn't realised how much his song could be enhanced. He wasn't the best at singing, but he wasn't bad. He could do so to show them what the song sounded like, but still, the band was in need of a singer.

After the session, they all put their instruments away.

'That was amazing,' said Henry.

'We should do a jam session at my parents' house this Sunday,' said Levy. 'I could also show you some stuff I've been working on. You should all come for a meal for Shabbat! Are you free Saturday for lunch? My parents would love to host you!'

'Sure,' replied Simon.

'Yeah,' replied Matthew and Henry, both of whom had never been to a Shabbat meal before.

'Why don't you ask Reuben to come?' suggested Levy.

'For what?' asked Simon.

'For lunch.'

'Really?' said Simon, now confused. He hadn't expected him to want to invite Reuben. He had been so used to his old friends not wanting him around, he assumed that his new ones wouldn't, either.

'Sure, why not?' said Levy. 'He seems like a nice fellow.'

'Er, sure,' said Simon.

Later that night, Simon mentioned the invitation to Reuben. He was delighted (although, admittedly surprised as well), and accepted happily.

CHAPTER XXXV

As they all lived in the same neighbourhood, there was more than one instance in which one of Simon's old friends could have appeared. That Wednesday, he caught sight of Asher walking up the other side of the street from the opposite direction. Simon wasn't sure whether he'd seen him as well. Either way, Asher disappeared down another street before they could acknowledge each other. Simon seriously thought the whole situation was silly. Hadn't anyone thought they'd cross paths at some point? Why wouldn't they have wanted to make peace? It would have made things much less awkward.

While going for a walk a few days later, he saw Adam coming up Golders Green Road towards him. He instinctively kept moving but it was too late. Adam locked eyes with him, came up to him, and said, 'Reuben?'

Simon was shocked. He hadn't thought of pretending to be Reuben again.

He'd long thought of Adam as malicious, but after everything Dan had told him, he was nearly sure he was unhinged and unscrupulous, maybe even dangerous. He then thought to defend Reuben's honour after his last encounter with him. He didn't want Adam to go on thinking that Reuben was so naïve as to believe that Simon would have actually said those damaging words about him, much less anything that would've come out of that reckless man's mouth.

'Yes, it's me,' answered Simon, wondering whether that would've qualified as a normal response. 'It's very unfortunate that Simon said those things about me.'

'Right,' said Adam, nodding with a sympathetic facial expression.

Simon was taken aback – and, admittedly, impressed – by his acting skills.

Then Simon caught sight of who else but Reuben approaching from behind Adam. Of all people!

'Simon?' called Reuben.

Adam turned around.

'Reuben,' corrected Simon, pointing at himself while Adam couldn't see his gesture.

'What are you doing here?' asked Reuben, looking suspiciously at Adam. 'Hello,' he said flatly to him.

'Reuben, hey,' said Simon.

'What?' said Reuben, now genuinely confused.

'I mean, Simon,' said Simon.

'Simon, what are you saying?' asked Reuben.

Simon blushed.

Adam looked at Simon contemptuously.

Simon felt like Adam was reading his mind. Somehow, he knew that Adam now knew. He knew it was Simon. He knew it had been Simon the last time he had seen him. He knew that Simon knew the lie Adam had told him. Simon had caught him in his own game, a feat Simon hadn't intended.

Adam left the scene, turning around and walking up the road, opposite the direction from which he had been walking when Simon had first spotted him, which made him seem directionless. Simon was left gazing after him in shock.

CHAPTER XXXVI

Simon figured that Levy and Asher weren't very close. Levy barely spoke about him, apart from a memory he'd share about them in yeshiva while growing up. He gathered that they had grown apart somewhat after yeshiva. Still, though he was tempted to ask whether Asher had ever mentioned him, he thought it was time to finally move on from his old friends. Maybe they were still in distress, but no one had contacted him, and they hadn't answered when he had initiated contact with them. Dan had briefly reappeared, but Simon hadn't heard from him since telling him he wouldn't let him join the band. Maybe his only objective had not been to reconnect, but to be part of the band after all.

Throughout that week, Levy shared some ideas he had for new music. He shared fragments of lyrics, melodies and series of chords he had come up with, as well as new material he had created that week, which Simon thoroughly enjoyed. He was happy to have another person actually composing new music, and music that he really liked on top of that.

That Thursday night, the four members of the unnamed band met in the living room with the intention of jamming and sharing any material they had composed.

Henry showed off some beats he had come up with. Matthew then led with some bass notes, which the others accompanied. Simon shared his song 'A New Year', which had some slight changes from the original version he had made some months back, which they all enjoyed. Levy played some of the songs he had shown Simon that week. They even came up with some interesting music, which Levy hummed his own melody to. Simon made sure to record it on his mobile, hoping to generate lyrics to it later.

'We need to come up with a band name,' announced Simon after they stopped playing music.

'The Iron Spaceship,' said Levy.

Simon looked at him in a funny way. There was nothing about the band that suggested anything about space.

'No,' Matthew thankfully said.

'The Players,' suggested Henry.

Simon thought that was too broad. He took out a sheet of paper and a pen to write down their ideas.

'The Pieces,' said Matthew.

'The Spare Ire,' said Henry.

'Four Wise Men,' said Levy.

Simon put the pen down.

'I don't think we're going to come up with a proper name tonight,' he said, thinking they were too tired after playing together for hours.

After they had put away their instruments, Henry turned to the others and said out loud, 'My, this Adam guy definitely seems like an interesting person.'

Simon froze as he was just about to head to the kitchen. He felt a certain weight of shock and fear in his chest. Why was Henry speaking positively about Adam?

'Yeah, he definitely does,' agreed Levy.

Simon felt like he was being cornered. So, they had all met Adam at some point, which made sense, because Henry had probably met him through Matthew, and Levy through Asher. At least Matthew was in the same boat as he was with regard to no longer associating with him and having witnessed what had occurred between them. Did he need to expose Adam for who he truly was? Was it his obligation to advise Henry and Levy to no longer associate with him? He had felt victimised by all the trouble and pain he had caused him. Now, even after actively avoiding him, as they were speaking about him, it felt as though his presence were creeping its way back into his life, his private life, here in his personal space in his own household, and that made him feel very uncomfortable. He suddenly feared that Adam would somehow ruin his plans of forming his own band now that he was being proactive about it just like he had rejected him from being in The Beis. Would he cause the destruction of this new band, too?

Simon kept thinking about this even after the others had begun talking about something else. What if Adam tried to take his players away from him? Would he try to form his own band with them? He was curious to know just how unscrupulous Adam was willing to be in that hypothetical scenario, though of course, that was the last thing Simon wanted to happen.

As they were leaving, and he escorted them to the door, Levy planning to spend time with Matthew somewhere else, and he turned to Simon and said, 'Can I speak with you for a minute?'

'Sure,' Simon said.

Levy took him to the kitchen while the others waited by the door.

'I heard something and I wanted to confirm it with you, whether it's true,' said Levy. 'Adam told me you once stole his guitar and sold it on the Internet.'

Simon looked at Levy, who looked as though he thought this were absurd, yet a part of him still thought it could possibly be true.

'No,' said Simon.

'Oh, I thought so,' said Levy, which granted Simon relief. 'I thought that was rather odd. I don't know. I've got to go, but we'll talk soon.'

'Great,' said Simon, watching him as he left the house, joining Matthew and Henry.

As he stood alone in the quiet house, he was left with several unanswered questions after Levy had so quickly gone. When had Adam told him that? For how long had he known him? From what it sounded like, Levy and Henry had spoken of Adam as if they had recently met.

He was left with several doubts and anxieties. Did Levy not trust him? What else was Adam telling him? Would he move out? Should he expose Adam? Was it his duty to let Levy and Henry know what had occurred between them? Would they recommend one of the former players of The Beis – Adam worst of all – to join? Should he confront Adam about his wicked ways?

But then, he thought about it. He remembered what Ezra had told him. Many worries were running through his mind, but this was all from Hashem. God was testing him.

Adam had exposed his former friends as untrustworthy. Matthew had been an exception, who remained loyal to him. Even now, Levy had sought to confirm with him whether the rumour was true. If Adam was spreading lies about him to Levy and Henry, he would've been testing their loyalty, and so far, Matthew and Levy had passed the test.

He also thought that Adam's personality would speak for itself. His behaviour would indicate to others whether he was trustworthy or not, and the truth would emerge eventually.

He understood that Adam must have been envious of him. He really had no idea why he had been so hostile towards him, but there was reason to believe it would have got worse. Someone – whether Dan, Asher, Levy, Henry or someone else – had been bound to mention to him that he was trying to form a band. Simon was now clearly in a better position than him. The Beis had been a failure, apparently in large part due to the way Adam had been managing the band. Still, that was not Simon's problem. Adam seemed to want to destroy, but Simon was only interested in building. He had had a difficult few months, but now he was hopeful that the idea of the band would work out. Maybe this wouldn't be his main source of income, but at the very least, he wanted to make music to perform for others so they would enjoy it, and to uplift their spirits. He wanted his life to improve, which he felt it was.

And finally, he had confronted Adam before, and nothing good had come of it, apart from the knowledge that it wasn't a good idea.

CHAPTER XXXVII

Simon and Ezra went to their fellow congregant's house for dinner that Shabbat. His name turned out to be Mr Aberman. He was in his late fifties. All of his children were away at yeshiva in Israel or had got married and moved out, except for his twenty-two-year-old son Zvulun who dined with them, along with Mrs Aberman.

It turned out to be a lovely meal. Mr and Mrs Aberman seemed to be caring and genuine people who wanted to know about Ezra and Simon. Mr Aberman and Zvulun both shared words on the weekly parsha, and Simon and Ezra would've showed off their knowledge too, but Mr Aberman and Zvulun had already mentioned the insights they had gained earlier that week when they had learnt Rashi together.

Simon was just finishing the main course when he sat back in his seat (he was at the end of the dining table opposite Mr Aberman) and admired the piano in the living room. He had noticed it before, but couldn't mention it as they had been in conversation after having arrived from synagogue.

'Does someone here play piano?'

'Yes, Zvulun does,' said Mr Aberman.

Zvulun smiled shyly.

'Really? How well?' asked Simon.

'I've played for quite a few years now,' said Zvulun.

'He's being humble. He's a great piano player,' said Mr Aberman.

'Simon's started a band,' mentioned Ezra.

Simon had never thought of having a pianist in the band. He had been fixated on finding a singer, the only missing piece for the group to be able to properly call itself a band, but he was open to having one and thought it would greatly enhance the sound. Also, Zvulun seemed like a kind, sincere person to have around.

'Oh, have you?' said Zvulun, sitting up.

'Yes, it's nothing so serious, more a side project for now, but I have started a band and I'm trying to find players.'

'How many have you got so far?' asked Zvulun.

'An acoustic guitar player – that's me – a bassist, drummer, and electric guitar player. We're just missing a singer. A pianist would be nice, though.'

'Why don't you play some music for Melaveh Malkah tonight?' suggested Mr Aberman to Zvulun.

Zvulun blushed as he looked down.

As it was Shabbat, they didn't speak so much more on the subject as it involved an activity that wasn't allowed, and instead focused on Torah-related subjects.

Simon had in mind, however, to approach Zvulun after Shabbat to possibly join the band.

The next day, Simon, Reuben, Matthew and Henry went to Levy's parents' house for lunch. It was a delightful time with much joy and laughter. Levy mentioned how much he enjoyed spending time with all the guys and would love to hang out together again. He also said wonderful things about Reuben. Simon appreciated how much Reuben was being included.

Melaveh Malkah was going to take place a few hours after Shabbat ended at Mr Aberman's house, so Simon decided to pass by his parents' house. There, they were having Melaveh Malkah themselves. They had leftover challah and other foods from seudah shlishit, the third Shabbat meal.

Mrs Jacobs was in the kitchen heating up water for tea.

Simon sat by his father at the dining table. He offered Simon challah, but not only was Simon still satisfied from seudah shlishit, he also wanted to save his appetite for Melaveh Malkah later.

'So, have you had any luck with your job search?' asked Mr Jacobs.

'No,' said Simon, sighing. 'I should probably keep searching for new jobs.'

'Well, what is it you'd like to do?'

The only thing that Simon wanted to do was play music for others to enjoy, and, thank God, now he was in a better position to be able to do so. So, he shrugged and said stubbornly, 'I want to work in music.'

'What?' replied Mr Jacobs, which caught Simon by surprise. 'Why didn't you say so? The headteacher of the school where I work is looking for a music teacher to teach guitar.'

Simon wondered if he was having trouble hearing.

'Would you be interested? I can contact him for you.'

Simon had to hold himself back from screaming his answer.

'Yes.'

'Oh, wonderful. I'll let him know, then.'

Simon couldn't believe it. He'd potentially found a day job in which he could utilise his talents and work in a field he was passionate about. He could have a steady income from a day job in music and work on his band during his leisure time. He knew he hadn't received the job yet, but he couldn't have thought of such a brilliant solution. If he got the job, he would be able to pay rent and stay in the house and live with Reuben and Levy.

Now Simon had another reason to be excited as he headed to Zvulun's house. He had been exchanging text messages with him and had indicated he'd like to have him play the piano for him. Zvulun was interested in potentially being part of the band.

Simon expected to have Zvulun play piano for him maybe after the meal, but he arrived there earlier than Reuben, and Zvulun was eager to play for him there and then.

He sat down by the piano and played instrumental versions of several Shabbat songs. Simon enjoyed his musicianship and asked him after playing about four pieces, 'Would you like to be a part of the band?'

To which Zvulun replied, 'Yes!'

So, that night, Simon found a fifth member for the band.

Reuben came later and they sat down to partake of the Melaveh Malkah meal.

'So, what do you do for work?' asked Mr Aberman.

'I'm actually looking for work,' responded Simon, 'but I may have found something. Hopefully, I'll have an interview soon.'

'Hatzlacha,' said Mr Aberman, wishing him success.

'What about you?' asked Simon.

'I run a kosher café right here on Golders Green Road. You should come visit sometime. Zvulun sometimes helps out. You may see him there.'

'Yes, you should,' said Zvulun, nodding.

'I should come by sometime,' said Simon.

CHAPTER XXXVIII

Rabbi Isaacs had spoken a little bit about gratitude during the morning service on Shabbat. That Monday, towards sunset, Simon was drinking a cup of tea in the living room when he thought about appreciation. What was he grateful for? he thought. He was grateful for Ezra, who was a kind and understanding friend and study partner, and he was looking forward to his study session with him later that night.

After their study session, Ezra turned to Simon, closing the book as they sat by the dining table, and asked, 'How are you?'

'Thank you for asking,' Simon had to say first, because there weren't so many people who asked him this question nowadays without him asking first, and genuinely wanting to know the full answer. 'I'm doing a little better. I'm just still a bit stressed about Adam and what he's been doing.'

Ezra nodded, looking down pensively as he rested his chin on his hand.

'I know this may be difficult to hear, but it doesn't seem like there's much you can do about it. He's going to go on doing whatever he wants. You may not be able to do it now, but you may just have to eventually forgive him, and if you don't want to forgive him, at least move on, because he's not going to change.'

Simon appreciated his honest advice.

'No, you're right,' he agreed. 'I can't say I'm in a position to forgive him because he hasn't apologised, and he's done much damage, but I admit that at some point, I do have to move on.'

'OK, but just remember that someone doesn't have to apologise in order for you to forgive him. You can choose to forgive for your own sanity. Only you have the power to set yourself free. Simon, I wouldn't want to see you suffering forever because of this.'

'No, you're right. What you're saying is true. I should forgive him at some point,' said Simon. 'Don't worry. I won't be suffering forever.'

Ezra nodded.

'OK,' he said.

'And thank you so much for listening and being there for me,' said Simon. 'It's really helped me a lot.'

'My pleasure,' said Ezra.

Simon embraced him. He held onto what had been a positive force in his life, even if he was a newcomer. He desired to focus on the people in his life who were there for him, and not focus so much on those who sought to hurt him.

He wasn't going to let his past ruin his present life. He was going to live a happy life – without a happy club.

CHAPTER XXXIX

Henry had also come over on Monday night as Simon and Ezra were learning Rashi's commentary on the parsha in the dining room. He mostly sat in the living room, listening while not understanding most of the concepts they were discussing, nor the context. Henry had been raised Anglican, but he and his family weren't particularly religious, and he had never read the Bible.

The house was spotless, and Simon didn't have to rush to move all the mess out of the rooms and pile them in some hidden corner before Ezra arrived. Fortunately for him, Levy was orderly.

After the lesson, Simon offered tea to Henry, who had been sitting patiently waiting for them to finish for twenty minutes.

'Cheers, mate,' said Henry, grinning as he took the teacup.
'Pleasure,' said Simon.

Henry took a sip and hummed in satisfaction.

'So, this is kosher tea?' he asked.

Simon and Ezra laughed.

'Yes,' said Simon.

Henry took another sip.

'It's quite good.'

'It should be more or less the same, apart from the milk, which is Chalav Yisrael – that means it was supervised by a Jew,' said Simon.

The three of them chatted for a few minutes, and Ezra eventually left.

'I've spoken with Adam recently,' said Henry.

'Oh,' uttered Simon, before going into paralysis.

'He said the most bizarre thing,' said Henry, looking away and laughing anxiously. 'He said you broke one of his instruments.'

Henry kept laughing.

Simon was waiting, wondering if he had finished.

'He said you were angry and smashed his guitar,' he said.

Simon wasn't so emotional. He barely reacted. Normally, he would've become anxious at such an utterance and eager to prove his innocence, but he didn't try now. He just sat there. He was a bit surprised by how mildly he reacted. He realised all of this was lunacy. It wasn't real. Sure, it was all stemming from God. For whatever reason, He had put Adam into his life to tell Henry this. What the reason was, Simon didn't know. Maybe it was a test.

'I spoke to Matthew about it,' continued Henry. 'We both thought it was silly. We knew it couldn't be true. I could never picture you angry.'

Henry was clearly blessed.

'Thank you for not believing that,' said Simon.

Simon realised that he could now confide in Henry. He wouldn't believe false rumours. He was now happier he was in the band.

He went to bed relatively early that night. He had an interview scheduled with the headteacher of the school where his parents worked. Never would he have thought that he was destined to follow in his parents' footsteps – to their place of work.

As he got dressed the next morning, fastening his navy-blue tie around the collar of his white shirt with the aid of his bedroom mirror with Patrick sitting beside him by his feet, he couldn't help but think about Adam and how pathetic he was. He barely had any compassion for him; he made it difficult because of how hostile he was. What was it about him that merited such special treatment, so much attention from someone he barely saw, nor wanted to?

How empty was his life that he had to spend so much time spreading false rumours about *him*? Had he done something to him, or said something? Couldn't he realise that others were starting to see him for who he was? Maybe he was envious because Simon was starting his own band, but even before, when Adam had rejected him from his former band, he had been saying negative things about him. He shook his head. He didn't want to think about it anymore. It was a puzzle he couldn't solve. And if he kept trying to, he might go mad. Adam was self-important, because he was only important to himself. That way, he could be important to somebody.

He put on his suit, donned his coat, scarf and hat, and set off for the interview.

The interview was a success. He quite enjoyed it, as the headteacher was very warm and friendly. He said he thought he would be a good fit, and he admired his passion for music. He said he would hire him for the job.

After shaking his hand, thanking him, and leaving, Simon was still comprehending what had just happened. He had just received a job – in music. He would now have a steady income related to something he enjoyed. So many of his problems had just been solved. He was so relieved by the good news.

Though he was bursting with joy internally, the streets of Golders Green were calm and quiet on this ordinary Tuesday morning. He wanted to shout with joy, but he didn't want others to think he was mad. He then thought to tell his parents, but he had already crossed the street, and they were teaching.

He really wanted to tell somebody. As he walked down Golders Green Road, he thought to pass by Mr Aberman's café. Maybe Zvulun would be there and he could share the good news with him.

As Simon walked outside on that cloudy day, he realised he had so much to be grateful for. There were so many positive things in his life. Apart from the thrilling job offer he had just received, he was starting to get to know many people in the community. It was nice to have met the Abermans, as well as Henry. He had reconnected with Reuben, he was becoming close with Ezra, Matthew, Henry and Levy, he had two parents who cared about him, his grandparents were alive and well, he had a brilliant rabbi who gave priceless advice and endless amounts of Torah wisdom, he got to stay in his house, and the list went on and on. He was truly blessed.

He approached the café and saw through the windows that Zvulun was working there. There were some customers inside.

Simon slowly made his way towards Zvulun as he chatted with a customer, two other employees around him taking people's orders and handing them cups of coffee and pastries.

When he saw Simon, Zvulun grinned and greeted him.

'I got the job,' said Simon.

'Wow, mazal tov!' said Zvulun, his face filled with joy.

'Thank you,' said Simon, smiling. 'Busy day today?'

'Sort of. It's pretty normal for a Tuesday morning,' said Zvulun.

They spoke for a bit. Simon looked around and saw a young man sitting on a chair close to the windows reading. There was a long, black case sitting horizontally on the floor beside his chair. He noticed he was reading sheet music.

The band still needed a singer. Simon hadn't been sure when or if he would find one. He disliked the idea of having to approach Dan to sing in the group. No, he thought, he'd never have any of his former friends join his band. He'd rather take vocal lessons and sing himself. Maybe one of his other band members could do the same, too.

By this point, no one was queuing anymore. The café had become a bit quieter. The other employees conversed now that the customers' orders had been received, some of the customers who had just been served took their seats at the tables by the wall, and another pair of customers walked out of the café with their food and beverages.

'Do you know him?' Simon asked Zvulun softly, looking at the young man.

'No,' answered Zvulun.

'Ever seen him here before?'

'First time here, as far as I recall.'

Simon approached the young man. It was then when he realised how desperate he had become in his search for a singer. He'd never usually strike up a conversation with a stranger at a café, unless he was drunk on Purim and had no friends around.

'Excuse me,' said Simon, 'sorry, I've noticed you've got what looks like a musical instrument here. May I ask what you play?'

The young man fixed his glasses over his long nose. The frames of the glasses were rectangular. He had a very soft voice.

'I've got a clarinet.'

'Oh, do you play the clarinet?' asked Simon, then realised what a stupid question that was. The young man was so softspoken, he felt the need to be soft and gentle in return. He was waiting for him to say something along the lines of: 'No, I actually don't. I simply carry around a clarinet in a case for fun. It cost me money, but there are many benefits, including building more muscle one arm at a time.'

'Yes, I do play the clarinet. I give private lessons.'

'And what's your name?' asked Simon, recovering slightly.

'Issachar Horowitz,' he said, offering Simon his hand. 'What's yours?'

'Simon Jacobs,' he replied as they shook hands. 'I actually teach music and I've started a band,' he said rather pompously.

'You teach music?'

'Yes, well,' said Simon, stuttering, 'I actually haven't started yet. I just got the job today. I'll be starting tomorrow.'

'Oh, mazal tov,' said Issachar. 'And you said you've started a band.'

'Yes, and we're in need of a singer, though I think we could also use a clarinet player.'

Simon was wondering if he was starting an orchestra instead of a band. Still, he'd be open to having a clarinet player in his rock band – or whatever genre would come out of it. He already liked Issachar.

'I actually sing, too,' said Issachar, smiling almost as though he secretly enjoyed this more than playing the clarinet.

'Do you?'

'Yes.'

'Do you mind singing something for me?'

Simon knew he might be too shy to do so, but he fancied the idea of his quest to find a vocalist ending there and then.

Issachar cleared his throat. He then sang the tune of 'Lecha Dodi'.

Within seconds, Simon knew he had found the singer he'd been looking for. He flowed through the notes gracefully.

Issachar stopped after the third repetition of the refrain.

'I sometimes like to lead services at my shul,' he said, meaning synagogue.

'That was brilliant,' said Simon. 'Would you like to be part of the band?'

'Sure, I would.'

'Fantastic,' said Simon.

They exchanged contact details. The band now had a singer and clarinet player, and it was six people strong. As Simon exited the café, he was amazed at how successful Hashem had made his endeavours. He now had a proper band and a job.

He crossed the street. This was clearly an opportune day. He was excited for what the future had in store for him. He thanked Hashem for all the wonderful things that were happening. He truly felt like he was on top of the world. There was a slight drizzle that almost seemed to float in the air. It only lasted a few minutes, and the clouds remained.

He then thought about Adam, but not in the same way he usually thought of him. There was less fear this time. He wasn't as angry. He was ready to forgive him. Adam had never asked for forgiveness and might never do so, but Simon took in a deep breath as he walked down the road and exhaled, looking up towards the sky, and he forgave him. He forgave him for everything he had done, which he no longer wished to think about. He wasn't sure whether the sudden shift that had occurred within him was a result of his newfound success in finding a job, or his happiness after finally finding a singer for the band, thus completing it, or maybe it was all Hashem's grace. He couldn't tell, but it had happened. He almost felt a little sorry for Adam. Whatever evil he was committing was Adam's problem, not his. He felt lighter. He let it go. He was moving on.

A little further down the street, Simon slowed down and came to a halt. There was a familiar face standing on the corner amidst the groups of pedestrians flowing in different directions. It was Adam. Simon didn't move. Adam only stared at him with his dark, callous eyes. His face had no expression, no mark of delight, no trace of despair, no frustration nor surprise to see him. It was almost as if his eyes were looking through him, or just past. They appeared empty of all emotion. Though his arms were covered in the sleeves of his coat, Simon didn't have to check whether they were covered in goosebumps. He felt a brief wave of discomfort, but he felt protected by being outside in public. This was a lost soul, he thought. There was not much else he knew about him. All this seemed to last forever, but it took place in a matter of seconds.

He then turned right and disappeared.

Simon never saw him again.

CHAPTER XL

Simon couldn't help thinking a great deal about this last encounter with Adam. He didn't know why, but whenever he did, he felt full of guilt, as if he had done something wrong. He couldn't explain why.

On Wednesday of that week, he started his job giving guitar lessons to kids, and he thoroughly enjoyed it. They were very enthusiastic to learn the instrument, and some of them impressed him with the skills they already possessed.

His parents were very pleased that he was now working, and that he was enjoying his job on top of that.

Before Shabbat had started, he had had a conversation with Chaim, who was doing well, thank God. They had agreed that they should see each other soon. Chaim would try to come visit. Whether he would or not that spring, Simon thought to visit him in the summer. They also thought to start learning a new tractate together, like before, and they settled on the tractate of Shabbat. They would start learning Sunday night.

Simon enjoyed living with his housemates. Issachar was thinking of moving in next month, which would've been amazing, not only because of his easygoing personality, Simon thought, but because he would get to live with two of his bandmates.

They had had a brief jamming session on Thursday night at Simon's house, when he had introduced everyone to each other and they had played some music. They had all accepted Issachar into the band, and they all seemed to get along tremendously well. Everyone had a good time together. The band had now been formed.

Friday had carried the Tenth of Tevet, which had been a fast day, which meant that Simon had faced added pressure to prepare food – with the help of his housemates – for everyone to enjoy, though their satisfaction was easily achieved after a fast. As Matthew and Henry weren't Jewish, they hadn't fasted, but enjoyed the food anyway.

Now it was Shabbat. It was Friday night, and Simon had invited his housemates, Ezra, Matthew, Henry, Zvulun and Issachar to partake in a Sabbath dinner. They had all come back from synagogue. Matthew and Henry had joined Simon at his synagogue for the afternoon and evening services out of curiosity, looking lost the whole time, and understandably so.

Now, they were all feasting and celebrating together. Simon couldn't have thought of a better way to spend Shabbat dinner than with his friends. He appreciated that they were all here feasting and celebrating with him.

As they all ate, Simon stared absent-mindedly at the bowl of rice before him, reflecting. His life had changed so much.

He had been working at a job he hadn't liked, he had had friends who had possessed much potential for betrayal, and one of his true friends had been taken hostage by terrorists. Now, he was feasting with friends who truly cared about him, he was working at a job he enjoyed, he had his own band, and Chaim had been freed. His life had felt like a nightmare, and now it felt like a miracle. He didn't know how he had got through it. Clearly, Hashem had helped him a great deal. He was living a happier, more meaningful life.

Interestingly enough, it had been Adam who had helped him get here. If it hadn't been for him, he probably would've formed a band with members whose loyalty was questionable. In a way, he owed him a great deal of gratitude, though of course, that wouldn't be expressed verbally to him.

And with regard to friends, he wasn't quite sure whether Reuben had been successful in acquiring new friends on his own, but he wouldn't have to worry about that, because Simon's friends had accepted and appreciated him as he was. Simon's friends were Reuben's friends.

'The food is great,' remarked Issachar.

'Yeah, everything is delicious,' said Henry.

'Thank you, it was all with help from Reuben and Levy,' said Simon, smiling as he saw Reuben and Levy blush.

'You're always so positive,' said Matthew. 'How are you so happy?'

'Thank God,' said Simon, 'I've got good friends and family, faith, a great job, and a meaningful life.'

About the author

Joseph Estevez is the author of two poetry collections, a short story collection and a novella. He published his debut novel *Isaac Abrams* in 2023.

Printed in Great Britain
by Amazon